# You Weren't Watching

Stephanie Hazeltine

YOU WEREN'T WATCHING

Edited: Penny Carroll

Cover design: Elle Maxwell Designs

Published by Hazeltine Publishing

eBook – 978-0-6455756-4-4

Paperback – 978-0-6455756-5-1

To my beautiful children,
I will never take my eyes off you

# Trigger Warnings

Note to my readers:

This book includes kidnapping and references to stalking, human trafficking, addiction, custody battles and mental health issues. It also details the event of a child in anaphylactic shock.

# Prologue

I lost my daughter once, at the supermarket. I'd been distracted while I paid for my groceries and when I looked up, she was gone. It was only a few seconds before I found her playing on the coin-operated kiddies' ride out the front, but it took my breath away.

Today was different, but it started like any other day.

***

'Babe, don't forget I've got cricket training after work tonight,' my husband says around a mouthful of cereal. 'Also, I've got a delivery arriving today.'

My head snaps up from my phone. 'Do I need to be here for it?'

'If you don't mind. They'll leave it at the shed door but it's work stuff and it costs a fortune, so just drag it inside if you can.'

'No probs,' I say, keeping my voice light as a wave of anxiety washes over me.

He leans over and gives me a kiss. 'Call me when the munchkin wakes up.'

'Will do.'

Our daughter has taken to sleeping in, which means he doesn't always see her before he leaves for work. Apparently neither of them can truly start their day until they say good morning to one another, so now we FaceTime while she eats her breakfast. No matter what he's doing, he always picks up to say a quick hello. It's very sweet.

He's been gone half an hour when my toddler enters the kitchen, dragging a doll behind her.

'Morning, munchkin.'

'Hi, Mama.' She smiles. 'Breakfast.'

I pass her a bowl of cereal and make the call.

'Daddy!' she says, milk dripping down her chin.

'Good morning, sweetheart. I like your milk beard today.'

She giggles and pokes her tongue out to try and lick up the milk.

'Missed a bit!' he teases. 'Have a good day, honey. I love you.'

'Luvoo, Daddy. Bye.'

I turn the camera to face me.

'Thanks, babe. Don't forget the delivery,' he says.

I roll my eyes. 'Yes, I know. See you later.'

I hang up and turn to my daughter. 'What do you want to do today?'

'Outside!' she yells, Weetbix spraying from her mouth.

'Okay, once you're dressed, we'll head out.'

'With cream and hat, Mummy.'

'Of course. Good girl for remembering. We'll get your hat and sunscreen, too.'

***

By midday the delivery still hasn't arrived and the knot that's been sitting in my stomach since breakfast pulls tight at the thought. I don't like allowing strangers onto our property. I'm always worried that I'll be recognised, even here in a new town like Huntley.

I shove the worry aside and start whisking fresh eggs from our chooks for lunch. The munchkin loves collecting the eggs each morning and always thanks our hens as we do it. Such a sweetheart.

'Lunch is ready!' I call through the kitchen window.

The mention of food is a sure-fire way to get my always-hungry daughter inside. She would spend hours playing in the yard if her grumbling tummy didn't intervene.

I watch her run up the lawn with a hilarious toddle that makes her bum wiggle dramatically. She stumbles, falls and squeals 'uh-oh' before getting back up. Other three-year-olds have mastered running and jumping by now but my girl didn't have the same start in life as most kids. I will always feel guilty about that.

She eats her lunch while chatting to her dolls propped up on the table in front of her. I love cooking for my little girl because I could serve up a Vegemite sandwich and she'd appreciate it as though it was a five-course degustation. Today's omelette is no different. She eats every bite, totally unfazed by the vegetables I've snuck into it.

It's mid-afternoon when a truck finally pulls into the long driveway, kicking up dust behind it. It has a white cabin and a dark purple trailer emblazoned with the initials 'BM' in yellow. My husband often has supplies sent to the house—such is the nature of being self-employed—but I haven't seen this truck before.

I point the driver in the direction of the shed and glance at my daughter playing in the front yard. She's running around swinging her new butterfly net, shrieking with joy despite catching nothing.

'Sweetie,' I call, 'I'm just going to unload some things in the shed.'

'Okay, Mummy,' she sings, swatting her net over a bed of flowers.

The driver climbs out of the cabin. He's wearing sunglasses and a purple cap the same colour as the truck.

'Delivery for PJ Works?' he asks.

'Yes,' I say, hurrying past him to open the shed. The less time he spends with his eyes on me, the better.

The man unloads several boxes, dumps them at the roller door and shoves a clipboard in front of me. 'Sign here.'

I do as I'm told and turn to sort the boxes so there's no chance of any small talk. The truck is just leaving the property as I lock the shed behind me.

***

'Honey!' I run around the deck that circles our house, yelling so loud my voice cracks. 'Where are you?'

My stomach is rolling and my chest is tight; I can't seem to get enough air. She's no longer in the garden chasing butterflies. It isn't unusual for her to lose interest in an activity and find something else to do but she knows she has to be in view of the house. If she can't see the house then I can't see her, and she always follows this rule. But this time, I wasn't in the house. I wasn't watching.

Dread slams into me. If she spotted a butterfly and kept chasing it, who knows where she could be. My knees buckle and I grip the balustrade to steady myself, give myself a moment to think.

I know what I have to do. I grab the keys to the ride-on mower and sprint to the garage. My hand is trembling so much it takes a few tries to insert the key in the ignition and turn it. The engine clicks. Click. Click. Click.

*Come on.* I kick the mower in frustration. Taking a deep breath, I turn the key again. It starts.

I drive far too quickly to the front of the property. This'll be the fastest way for me to search the whole place. If my husband saw the speed I was travelling he'd have a fit. But our baby girl is missing. There's no time to spare. I grip the steering wheel as the mower hits the gravel, my body lurching side to side.

When I get to the end of the driveway, I curse. *Bloody truck driver.* He's left the gate open despite the very clear sign saying to keep the gate shut at all times. There's no way she would wander out the front gate, though. Even as I remind myself that, I swallow back the lump rising in my throat.

From the front gate, there are two driveways. One leads straight to the house, the other follows the creek along the side of the property to the shed. The creek is a sore point for my husband and I because I've been nagging him since we moved in to put a fence up beside it.

I take the driveway to the shed. She knew I was unloading things there, maybe she went looking for me. Big gum trees line the gravel drive, partly obscuring the creek just beyond. We've had some big rainfalls recently so the water is moving quickly. Usually I find the sound relaxing but today it makes my heart pound. I've never noticed just how fast and frantic the creek runs.

As I near the shed, a flash of yellow catches my eye. I edge closer. It's her butterfly net, lying beneath a tree just metres from the bank.

I scream her name as I jump off the mower and hurtle towards the rushing water.

PART I

# Chapter 1

## Charlotte

'Mummy, train!' Imogen points to the third train that has passed us in the last few minutes.

'Yes, Immy. Another one,' I say in that voice parents use when they're pretending to be equally excited by the mundane happenings that thrill their child.

It's one of the reasons we always come to this park. My almost three-year-old loves watching the trains pass during the morning rush. Lately we've been leaving the house early because Melbourne is in the middle of some never-ending heatwave and being outside after 10 a.m. is just a sweaty mess. Plus, it times nicely with Jordy's morning nap.

The train toots its horn as it passes and Imogen bounces up and down on her trike seat. When she's satisfied the train is gone, she starts moving her little trike along the track again. I follow behind, pushing Jordy in the pram, thankful that the noise never wakes him.

After I had Imogen I'd come to this park because the dogs didn't need a leash, so I could easily manage the pram and our two labradors. Now, we come here for the trains while our poor dogs sit at home, missing the old days. I don't think I could juggle a pram, a bike-riding toddler and two free-running dogs. It's a betrayal that their sad little eyes remind me of each time they cuddle up to me for a belly rub on the couch.

As we round the corner at one end of the park, a woman in a black sports bra and small black shorts jogs towards us. Her midriff is tanned and toned and I immediately think of my postpartum body and how far from ready it is to be flaunted in public. The woman has long, dark hair tied in a ponytail and sunglasses that bounce up and down on her face as she runs.

I used to be a runner before the kids came along and I desperately want to get back into it. But my pelvic floor, gigantic postpartum chest and complete and utter lack of time has made it impossible. I watch with envy as she approaches, probably staring a little too closely.

'Great job, mama!' she calls to me.

I smile. People don't say hi often enough to strangers, let alone pay random people compliments.

'Thanks,' I say as she runs past.

She turns so that she's running backwards. 'I know how hard it is to get kids out of the house. You're doing so well.'

She spins back around and takes off before I can say anything else. I'm still grinning when another train rolls past and Imogen goes through the pointing and shrieking routine all over again.

Little comments like that mean a lot to me. Sometimes I feel like I can barely make it through the morning without crying or getting frustrated at the kids. But today is off to a great start.

Imogen waves goodbye to the train and we continue our walk, this time with a little more spring in my pram-wielding step.

# Chapter 2

## Sloane

*Seriously, what did I ever see in that jerk?*

Frankie waves from the backseat of Tarkyn's car. It's her week with her dad. He keeps his eyes straight ahead as he drives past. Can't even look at me. Probably doesn't want another glimpse of what he's missing out on.

I pause before going back inside, admiring the reflection of my legs in the window by the front door. I work bloody hard for this body. I wouldn't be surprised if he regrets letting it go. And for who? Goody-two-shoes Janie Benson. *Janie.* Blergh. Even her name sounds boring. Tarkyn says she's 'much better mother material' than I am. Isn't carrying a baby for nine months, pushing her out of a tiny hole and then looking after her the definition of mother material? Apparently not.

Tarkyn had outrageous expectations of me as a mother. Remain healthy and lose the baby weight, but don't train too hard. Bond with Frankie as much as possible, but get back to work—we couldn't possibly all live off his wage. Don't work too much, but enrol Frankie in the most expensive sensory classes. I was set up to fail.

When I get inside, I tidy up Frankie's toys. Unlike most playrooms, it'll stay neat for the next week. Though, I find comfort in the mess. It means my baby is with me.

As I potter around the kitchen, I find the tins of supplements that I've been giving Frankie. I was meant to pack them for her.

I shoot off a text to Tarkyn.

*I forgot to pack Frankie's supplements. I'll drop them off in the morning.*

A text comes back almost immediately.

*What does a two-year-old need supplements for? Don't worry about it.*

*Seriously?* Just because he was happy to let his health go and embrace the 'dad bod' doesn't mean he can neglect our child's health.

*The supplements ensure she isn't missing out on any essential nutrients for her immune system, gut health and brain development. I don't know what she's eating while she's at yours but additional nutrients won't hurt.*

Let's see him try and rebut that.

His response comes through moments later.

*Don't bother coming by tomorrow. I'm working and Janie is taking Frankie for a girls' day out.*

I gasp. It's like he just shoved a blade into my heart and twisted it. It kills me knowing Janie will be having a day with *my* daughter.

*Frankie has childcare.*

Plus, doesn't Janie work too? They met when Tarkyn started a new job. They both teach at the same school. She must have excellent staffroom banter because he was at the school only two months before he left me for her.

*She's not going to childcare this week. Janie has taken a few long service leave days so that she can bond with Frankie, just the two of them.*

Bond. Just the two of them. Bond. The way he claims I haven't done. I want to demand a police check or some evidence of her competence to look after a child. But her day job already requires all of these things and I've been reminded on more than one occasion how *maternal* and *gentle* Janie is. I don't think I've ever been described like that.

Even my boss has criticised my bedside manner. I work part-time as a physiotherapist in a hospital and my patients are often recovering from major surgery, but they don't need me to mother them and tell them that everything is going to be okay. They need me to work them hard, make them move, get my hands into those niggly areas. No pain, no gain, right?

'Did you just tell Mrs Carson to toughen up?' my boss asked me one day.

'Yeah, she was slacking off at the end of our session,' I'd responded, unsure what the problem was.

'She's eighty-three with a new hip, Sloane. Go easy.'

'She'll thank me when she's walking good as new again in a few weeks.'

These conversations happen a lot with my boss but I'm yet to have a patient who doesn't achieve their recovery goals. Sometimes tough love is just what they need.

I stare at Tarkyn's response on my phone. He's baiting me. He knows that his message would hurt.

Tapping at my screen, I smile. This will piss him off.

*How lovely. Also, forgot to mention, Frankie has had diarrhoea for a few days. Just keep an eye on it.*

She hasn't. But nothing gives a parent anxiety like the anticipation of gastro symptoms.

*Have fun, Janie.*

\*\*\*

No one can prepare you for the loneliness of a custody arrangement. The transition from family unit to single parent with every second week entirely alone is hard. Gut-wrenchingly hard.

The first day without her is the easiest. I have a routine: every second Sunday, when Frankie leaves, I go for my long run—at least twelve kilometres. I switch on some music or a podcast, take in the sights of the river trail, smile at other runners or cyclists and breathe that fresh air like it's an addictive drug.

But when I get home, it hits. The silence. The emptiness.

I've had a few Tinder dates here and there but let's face it, it's Tinder. We're all there for a good time, and honestly, sometimes calling it that is a stretch. It doesn't cure the loneliness.

Finding someone I actually want to see again is proving difficult. Not that there's been many second date offers. I've had a few of these texts:

*Sloane, you're a total ten, but I'm not ready to be involved with someone with kids.*

I thought being up front about Frankie was the best approach but it turns out she's the ultimate cockblocker. Lucky she's cute.

So tonight it's just me and my foam roller, again. Not the worst date. It hits the right spot and when it does, it feels great.

# Chapter 3

## Charlotte

J ordy and I get to the park earlier than usual. Imogen is at childcare today and I thought it best to get our walk in before today's predicted thirty-eight degree peak. Imogen goes to a childcare not far from our house. It's a gorgeous little place and she started when she was almost one. She settled in easily. I don't know why I worried so much about the transition.

Those few months before I fell pregnant again with Jordy were amazing. On the days I didn't work, I took Imogen on all sorts of adventures: the zoo, the library, hobby farms and every playground recommended on the mummy blogs I read. Pregnancy was hard, though. I slowed down, so our adventures slowed down too. Imogen never complained but she became even more excited to go to childcare. Broke my heart a little, even though I was grateful that she liked it there.

Now I'm filled with guilt that I haven't done all the activities I did with Imogen with Jordy. He doesn't get the baby swim lessons and sensory play sessions because it's all the more overwhelming and tiring with two kids. I'm constantly doubting myself. *Am I a good enough mother to have two kids? Is it normal for the second child to miss out on so much?*

I manage just one lap of the park before the early morning sun becomes too hot and Jordy starts to grizzle. On the way to the car,

Jordy turns it up a gear and starts screaming. I try to put his dummy in and he spits it out. I offer him a toy and he throws it on the ground. I check his nappy and it's clean.

'Sorry, bud, but if it's food you want, you'll need to wait until we get home. It's only five minutes.'

I cringe at myself as I say it. It feels weird chatting to a seven-month-old baby who gives no response. Now I'm speaking as though he understands units of time, how ridiculous. My talking only seems to make him more upset and in my haste to get him in the car, I make a mess of putting down the pram and tip everything out of my bag in the process.

'Here, let me help you,' says a voice behind me.

I turn to see the lovely woman who ran past me the other day. Her face is flushed and covered in a film of sweat. It seems she didn't quite beat the heat, either. She hands me Jordy's dummy, which he'd managed to toss a few metres out of the pram. Not strong enough to lift some of his toys but can throw a dummy like he's a fast bowler.

'Thanks,' I say.

'No worries. A grizzly baby in the heat. I know the feeling.'

I nod. 'When the weather is like this, he just wants food all day long.' I keep collecting things from the ground around my car, stuffing them back in my bag.

'Where's your daughter today?' she asks.

'Imogen's at childcare.' I immediately curse myself for saying her name, remembering my mum's lectures about privacy and stranger danger.

'Rosewood ELC?'

I look up at the woman. My mouth hangs open a little but I can't find any words. How does she know that?

'You should see your face.' She lets out half a laugh and holds up an envelope. 'You dropped this.'

It's the enrolment forms for Imogen's kindergarten. The centre handed them to me this morning.

My laugh is forced. I hope she doesn't sense my discomfort. She's been nothing but friendly the two times I've seen her. Friendly and helpful.

'Anyway,' I say. 'I better get this little guy home for a feed.'

'Of course, see you round,' she says.

I expect her to continue on her run but when I finally slide into the car and glance in the rear-view mirror she's still standing on the kerb, watching as I drive away. A wave of nervous energy ripples through me and my fingers close tight around the steering wheel. Then Jordy lets out an ear-piercing wail and my thoughts about the woman disintegrate.

# Chapter 4

## Sloane

On the weeks I don't have Frankie, I start every day at the gym. I feel my best when I'm exercising.

My mum died from a stroke just before my tenth birthday. She was only forty-two. Dad became very focused on our health after that. He educated himself and me on macronutrients and which foods were best for lowering our risk of heart problems or stroke. He also started taking me to the gym, where I'd run alongside him on the treadmill, and he enrolled me in all sorts of different sports. His passion for health and fitness rubbed off on me, although some people call it an obsession rather than a passion. An unhealthy obsession. But how can an obsession with being healthy be unhealthy?

This morning I opt for the 6 a.m. boxing class. Perfect for releasing built-up tension and I'm not hurting anyone when I picture Janie's annoying little face on the boxing bag as I slam a right hook into it. It's going to be a long day distracting myself from thoughts of that woman 'bonding' with Frankie.

I shower at the gym and head straight to work. Rehabbing patients in the hospital is definitely not my dream job. What I really want to do is get injured athletes back on their feet, help them achieve goals that they thought weren't possible anymore. But whenever I look into jobs at sporting clubs, they're always full-time, never flexible. My dream is on hold until Frankie goes to school. In the meantime, I'm helping average Joes get used to new hips or knees and listening to them complain about how hard their lives are.

I pull my shoulders back as I walk through the hospital's double doors, trying to transform into positive, supportive Sloane with a slightly more acceptable bedside manner.

Looking at my schedule, I'm pleased to find it's not all geriatrics or middle-aged men who pulled a dumb stunt over the weekend and wound up in surgery. My list has a name I know very well. Jett Acres. I went to high school with him and he plays seniors at Rosewood Football Club. Seriously attractive, too. His file says he's had a knee reconstruction. At last, something to take my mind off Plainey Janie.

The nurses are clearing the lunch trays when I drop into Jett's room.

'Jett Acres. Long time, no see.'

He smiles. 'Hey. I didn't think there'd be too many physios named Sloane. Was hoping it'd be you.'

My cheeks flush.

Jett's sitting up in the bed wearing a white T-shirt and tiny footy shorts. I force myself to look away from his toned thighs and calves and focus on Jett's file.

'How's it feeling?' I nod towards the knee strapped into a huge brace.

'Not bad. I've stopped most of the painkillers so I'm doing pretty well, I reckon.'

What a breath of fresh air from the patients who tell me how great the Endone is and give me a look of horror when I mention they should start cutting back. I know that my patients need pain relief but why would you want to put toxins in your body for longer than necessary?

Dad hated how readily available drugs were. He claimed medication is just putting a Bandaid on the real issue. *If you take painkillers for a headache, you're not addressing the underlying problem,* he'd say. *Your body is telling you it needs something, perhaps water or nutrients.* I avoid medication at all costs. I didn't use any pain relief when Frankie was born.

'That's great,' I say, making a note on his file. 'Let's get you up and walking, then.'

His face pales. 'Haven't tried that yet.'

'Don't worry. I'm here to hold your hand.' *See, I can do caring bedside manner.*

Jett slowly swings his legs over the edge of the bed. I squat down in front of him so my eyes are level with his legs and run through a few mobility tests with both knees. I place a hand on his good knee to feel the movement of the joint and my palm tingles where his skin meets mine. I'm sure he can feel it too, based on the way he stares into my eyes and breathes deeply.

I need to focus. There's a difference between bedside manner and bedding a patient.

'Okay, that all looks pretty good.' I hold up a set of crutches. 'I want you to use these to help yourself stand up but I don't want you to completely weight bear through your good leg. I want a small amount of weight and movement going through the injured knee too.'

'I thought you said you were going to hold my hand,' he responds. Jett reaches for the crutches, his hand closing around my fingers.

We freeze, eyes locked. I'm standing over him, the crutches between us, his warm hand on mine. The air between us thrums with heat.

'Babe, are you about to walk?' calls a voice from the door. A stunning young woman with glossy, nut-brown hair bounces in.

We both drop our hands and the crutches clatter to the floor. I scramble to pick them up and offer them back to Jett, who takes them without looking at me.

'Did I miss it?' she says.

'No,' Jett says. 'I'm just about to take my first steps.'

'That's amazing.' She looks at me, beaming. 'Hi! I'm Georgie, Jett's girlfriend.'

'Sloane,' I say, breaking eye contact quickly. 'Okay, up you get.' My tone is harsh, sensitive bedside manner gone. Well and truly. I don't have time to be nice to a guy like this. Jett was absolutely flirting with me while his poor girlfriend was out there, probably paying half a day's wage for the exorbitant hospital parking.

I've got no time for cheaters. Not after what Tarkyn did to me.

It was all long work days and staff get-togethers and school camp, and before I knew it he was confessing to cheating on me with a colleague and packing his bags. When I'd stalked Janie on Facebook and clocked who I was competing with, I was furious. She's short, frumpy, with mousey brown hair. I'm fit, five foot ten, and my naturally blond hair and blue eyes make me look like a Victoria's Secret supermodel. At least, that's what Tarkyn used to say about me, back when we first met. And when I reminded him what he was leaving, he had the hide to tell me that's not what he looks for in a wife—or a mother.

He did me a favour, though. I loved Tarkyn, but I love my independence more. And he was holding me back. Now I can be a good mother *and* be an athlete, have a career and have some no-strings-attached fun with men who appreciate how hard I work to look like this. One week on, one week off.

By the time I'm finished with Jett, he's confidently standing on his crutches and moving slowly around his room. Georgie excitedly films it all. Apparently, Jett walking after elective knee surgery warrants an

Instagram story. I try to block out the sound of Georgie debating which emojis to use in the caption while I make the final notes on Jett's file.

'Thanks, Sloane,' Jett says as I leave.

I just nod and walk away.

# Chapter 5

## Charlotte

Emmett is late getting home from work, again. It isn't unusual. You don't get a huge amount of say over your shift end times as a paramedic. If there's a call-out ten minutes before you're due to finish and the next crew aren't there yet, off you go.

I both hate and love Emmett's job. The night shifts are hell, especially with the kids, and the weekend work is annoying. But, the holidays are pretty good and we get to have him home during the day a little more than the average nine-to-five job. Still, I feel an irrational prickle of annoyance on nights like this one, when I'm exhausted from juggling the dinner-bath-bed chaos on my own and he arrives just in time to kiss their sleepy faces goodnight.

'Are they in bed?' Emmett asks, dumping his keys on the kitchen counter.

'Jordy's asleep but Immy's reading to her teddies. You can probably sneak in there and give her a cuddle.'

I watch on the monitor as Emmett creeps into Imogen's room and she claps with excitement.

'Shhh,' he says. 'Jordy's asleep next door.'

'Shhh,' she mimics him, but her shushing is just as loud as her clapping.

I heat up Emmett's dinner for him and wait for him to come back.

'I could listen to her read all day,' he says with a laugh as he strolls into the kitchen.

Imogen's toddler reading is just her speaking adorable gibberish while turning the pages and occasionally throwing in proper words when she recognises something in the illustrations.

'I know, it's so cute,' I say, handing him a bowl of spaghetti. 'How was work?'

He shrugs. 'Same old.'

I always ask Emmett about his day but I never get much out of him. I don't like that he hides this side of himself. I've heard the stats about suicide rates in the profession, about the burnout and the stress, but I can't force him to talk. I just remind him daily that I'm here to listen and hope that he's finding some way to manage the trauma he's exposed to.

'How was *your* day?' he counters. He's shovelling pasta into his mouth as though he hasn't eaten all day, and he probably hasn't.

'Uneventful. Imogen had a good day at childcare. There's a new piece of artwork.' I gesture at the fridge where her latest masterpiece now hangs, secured with bright alphabet magnets. 'Jordy and I had a quiet day. Went for a walk. Tried to keep cool.'

'That sounds nice.'

I nod. I'm lucky to have these quiet days with Jordy. The walk had been pleasant until he grizzled and I struggled to get him in the car.

'Oh,' I say, suddenly remembering. 'We got the forms for Imogen's kindergarten.'

'Already?'

'I know. It's scary to think she'll be at three-year-old kindy next year.' I rummage around the nappy bag for the forms. 'Dammit. I can't find them.'

'When did you get them?'

'This morning when I dropped her off. They fell out of my bag at the park and this lovely woman picked them up for me.'

'And did she give them back?'

'Of course,' I say. Although, I can't really remember now. 'I think.' Surely she did.

'Just ask the centre for some new ones.'

'Yeah,' I respond, half tuned-out. I'm trying to recall the woman handing back the forms. Was she holding the envelope when she stood there, watching me drive away?

Emmett takes his bowl to the sink and interrupts my thoughts. 'I'm just going to take a slab over to Bailey's, say thank you. Be back soon.'

Bailey is our next-door neighbour. He's a twenty-something bachelor, lives alone, and seems to split his time equally between work, the gym and partying. He's the odd one out in our street, which is mainly young families and old couples, but Bailey is a popular guy. The dads love having a beer with him and the kids love playing with him because he can pick them up and throw them in the air with ease. Imogen adores Bailey because he pretends to use her as a barbell. She always begs him to bicep curl her or put her on his shoulders for a set of squats.

I have no idea what Bailey's job is but he was able to get his hands on a truck for Emmett when he needed to move some furniture for his parents last week. A slab of beer is an acceptable form of payment between most mates.

'Sure,' I say, my mind already back on the kinder forms. *Where are they?*

***

On Tuesdays I catch up with my mothers' group. We met more than two-and-a-half years ago when our toddlers were just weeks old. We were a group of eight but some mums have drifted out of contact because they've moved away or have returned to work full-time. Now there are just four of us who still get together regularly. There's Sloane, a glamorous blond who works part-time as a physio and, I swear, spends the rest of her time at the gym. She has a daughter, Frankie, but she shares custody fifty-fifty with her ex so Frankie only comes to our catch-ups every second week. I like that Sloane still comes without her, even though she must find it difficult. It'd be tough to watch all the kids playing together or hear us talking about them non-stop when your child isn't even living with you that week. But she puts on a brave face, most of the time.

Katya is the mum I'm closest to. She has two boys—Levi is the same age as Imogen and Oscar is just a bit older than Jordy—and they live only a few streets away from us, so our families spend a lot of time together. I'm certain I wouldn't have survived the first few months of motherhood without Katya.

And finally, there's Iris, the supermum of the group. She has two-year-old Billy and newborn twins, Sadie and Lara. The kids are always dressed beautifully, never a spot of dirt, dribble or spew to be seen. Billy always has chopped fruit and salad wraps prepared in a cute little bento box, usually accompanied by some delicious home-baked good. I don't know how Iris finds the time to pack a lunch, let alone bake a batch of sweet potato brownies or zucchini slice, but she does. I bet she doesn't sleep.

This morning we meet at the small park near the community centre. Once upon a time we could do brunch, even mums-and-bubs movie theatre sessions. That was back when our babies were immobile, sleepy blobs. Now, they're active, snack-devouring, adorable monsters.

Imogen, Billy and Levi run straight for the playground, which is, thankfully, a fully enclosed space and designed with small children in mind. We don't have to chase down toddlers on the run or worry about them falling from great heights. We set up a blanket on the grass nearby and Jordy and Oscar roll around, grabbing toys, sucking on them and then swapping. Delightful. The twins sleep soundly in their pram.

'Of course, they never do this when we're at home during the day or, you know, at night-time,' Iris says.

'Typical babies, right?' Katya responds.

'Yeah, except there's two of them,' I point out. 'And you still look amazing and I could absolutely smash that carrot loaf you've packed for Billy. I don't know how you do it.'

Iris beams at me. She seems to derive a lot of joy from us acknowledging her feats as a mum. I wish she'd slow down and rest. She's going to burn herself out.

'Coffee. A hell of a lot of coffee.' Iris sighs. 'It wouldn't be so bad if they coordinated their wakings and feeds. But I swear they're doing it on purpose, tag teaming and making sure I never sleep.' She half laughs, almost manically.

When Iris first told us that she was having twins, I almost blurted out 'I'm so sorry' rather than 'congratulations'. I felt awful but I just couldn't imagine how I'd cope. Iris was pretty terrified to begin with but she joined some Facebook groups for mums of twins and by the time they arrived, she said she felt prepared, excited even.

'Speaking of coffee,' Sloane says. 'Who wants one?'

There's a cafe across the road and we usually take turns shouting a round.

'It's my turn this week,' Katya says.

'Well, just give me some cash and I'll get them. No Frankie today so it's easier if I go.' The corners of Sloane's mouth turn down and she glances at the kids on the playground.

We place our orders and Sloane heads to the cafe. Iris leaves the girls sleeping next to our blanket while she goes to settle a dispute over the swings.

'I'm worried about her,' I say to Katya quietly.

'Who? Iris?'

'No. Although, yeah, a bit, I guess. But I was talking about Sloane. I think she's struggling with the custody arrangement more than she lets on.'

'But she says she's loving it. She gets a whole week to herself for her training, and to catch up on sleep and work. I'd love a week off,' Katya says, rolling her eyes.

'Of course, we'd love *one* week to ourselves. But any more than that and we'd miss the kids like crazy. Sloane has a week to herself every other week. It'd be horrible being away from your child that often.'

'Want me to talk to her? She's roped me into going to Parkrun with her on the weekend. Apparently it's for everyone, beginners included.'

My eyes widen. 'Good luck with that. And no, don't say anything. I'll do it.'

I wish I was invited to Parkrun on the weekend. Not just because I want to get back into running but because I don't like being excluded. Knowing that they'll be catching up on Saturday without me puts my mind in overdrive. *Will they talk about me? Will they laugh at me?* It's completely insane and I have nothing to justify these thoughts, but I can't help it.

Sloane returns with a tray of coffees and we spend the next half hour discussing how I want to move Imogen into a bed so that Jordy can use the cot, the plans for Oscar's first birthday, and how Billy is adapting to having not one, but two new siblings. Sloane doesn't say much.

I'm about to ask her how she's doing when Iris pipes up. 'Did you see the update on that missing child in Huntley?'

Iris is obsessed with news and true crime stories. She follows court trials, listens to podcasts and fixates on serial killers. How she doesn't have nightmares, I don't know. I've heard a bit about the missing child but I try to avoid those sorts of stories. I don't need more fuel for my anxiety-driven fire.

'Yes,' Katya says, her voice soft. 'The girl was the same age as our toddlers.' She gazes at them on the playground. They're all completely unaware that the world can be such a dangerous, awful place.

'I haven't seen it,' Sloane says, and I stop myself from raising my eyebrows at Katya because I'm sure she's thinking the same thing as me—that Sloane doesn't watch television, she's too busy exercising or meditating. 'How long has she been missing?' she asks.

'Over two weeks. The police have stopped the search and the family have all but given up,' Iris says.

I shake my head. 'I don't know what I'd do. If they haven't found her, surely they keep searching.'

'The evidence they do have suggests she probably drowned in the creek on their property. Her body would be long gone.'

I shudder. Iris often speaks of horrible crimes like she's a detective working the case, but the thought of a small child being swept away like that—it takes all my willpower not to vomit right here on our picnic blanket.

'Subject change, please,' Sloane says and Katya and I nod in agreement.

Sloane launches into a story about a creepy patient she recently treated and I'm feeding Jordy when Imogen cries out from the playground. It's the kind of high-pitched '*Mummy!*' that makes your insides sink and your heart race. My boob is out and Jordy is not going to take kindly to an interruption. I try to keep him in position while I attempt to get up from the blanket.

'I'll go,' Sloane says. 'She's just fallen at the bottom of the slide.'

'Thanks.' I turn and sit back down so I can see the playground better. Jordy has barely registered that I've moved. He's far too interested in his lunch to notice.

Sloane scoops up Imogen and brings her over to me.

'Are you okay, sweetie?' I ask.

'Where does it hurt, Immy?' Sloane adds, and a spark of annoyance flares in me. Only Emmett and I call her that.

Imogen points to her elbow. She's stopped wailing but tears still streak her face and she's about two seconds away from blowing a snot bubble. Sloane lifts Imogen's arm and inspects it quickly before kissing it better. Then she fishes a tissue out of her pocket and cleans up her face.

My jaw clenches. I'm grateful that my friend is helping Immy while my hands are full, of course I am. I'm also weirdly jealous. *I'm* Imogen's mum. *I'm* the one who kisses her injuries and wipes her face. Once again, I'm having to pick one child over the other. Offer my best to one, while the other misses out.

'All better?' Sloane asks.

Imogen nods. 'Thank you.' She runs straight back to the slide, the memory of what hurt her in the first place seemingly forgotten.

Sloane smiles at me and I force down the envy and self-doubt and thank her.

'I hate that I miss all these things with Frankie,' she says. 'I bet Tarkyn doesn't even kiss her boo-boos better.'

Guilt floods my stomach. Of course, Sloane was just filling the hole that Frankie leaves in her life every time she stays with her dad. How could I be so insensitive?

One of the twins starts to cry and, for now, I'm saved from trying to work out what to say to Sloane. Iris picks up Sadie. Or is it Lara? I'd feel bad but I know even Iris has mixed up her identical twins more than once. I mean, I call Imogen 'Jordy' and vice versa all the time. How is a sleep-deprived parent of identical twins supposed to get it right?

'It's okay, honey,' Iris says, rocking the wailing bundle. 'Would someone mind holding Lara while I make her a bottle?'

*Lara. I was wrong.* Iris hands Lara to Sloane, who enthusiastically cradles her and hums a soft tune.

Iris starts making a bottle. I continue to feed Jordy. Katya is shouting warnings to the older kids about throwing stones. No one says anything to Iris but she suddenly launches into a defensive speech.

'I know, I know. I'm giving Lara a bottle. I can't keep breastfeeding anymore.' Her cheeks are reddening and she's blinking rapidly. 'There's always one of them on me. I need a break.'

All three of us stare in confusion.

She sighs. 'I know no one said anything but maybe you're thinking it. The twins are only a few months old and I've already stopped.'

'I wasn't thinking it,' I say.

'Neither was I,' adds Katya.

'Or me,' Sloane says. 'You've got to do what you need to do to survive. I had Frankie on formula straight away. I didn't have the energy to both breastfeed and train.' She pauses, her face scrunching up. 'A fact that Tarkyn happily pointed out to the judge during our custody dispute.' She hands Lara back to Iris, who has the bottle ready. 'Sorry, I didn't mean to make that about me.'

'It's okay,' Iris says. 'I don't even know why I felt the need to defend myself. Just seems like every other twin mum on Instagram is breastfeeding her thriving babies and wearing make-up and hitting the Pilates studio while I wear the same leggings I wore yesterday and I haven't washed my hair in over a week.'

'My youngest is nearly one, Iris, and I haven't washed my hair for a week, *and* I'm not wearing underwear under my leggings because I don't have any clean pairs,' Katya says, chuckling. 'Plus, the contents of your kid's lunchbox is enough to make any foodie jealous.'

'I second that,' I add. Secretly, I'm buoyed to hear that even Iris the supermum struggles. I know all too well how social media can be both your best friend and worst enemy. I can scroll and find a great post about toddler tantrums or a nutritious recipe for the whole family. Or, I can see an influencer flaunting her perfectly toned, tanned body and cradling her baby with the hashtags #mumlife and #sleptallnight. *Ugh.*

Iris smiles. 'Thanks, girls. At least all the awake time is giving me an excuse to watch that new true crime doco on Netflix.'

'No more dead people stories!' Sloane cries, and Iris laughs.

Eventually the older kids return from the playground, guided by their rumbling stomachs that desire only crackers and cheese and absolutely no fruit or vegetables. Once the kids are fed, we pack up and head home for naps.

Sloane helps me load the kids into the car, strapping Imogen in and talking to her sweetly. In the next car space, Iris juggles Billy and the twins and I wonder why Sloane felt the need to help me over her. Did I look like I was struggling? Did Sloane think I wasn't looking after Imogen properly after what happened in the playground?

As I start the car and wave goodbye to the other mums, I tell myself to forget it. Offers of help are not accusations of neglect. If it's not social media, it's our own paranoia making us question ourselves.

This mum gig really is hard.

# Chapter 6

## Sloane

I don't have a lot of friends. Besides Frankie, I put myself first. I don't drink alcohol, which is apparently some crime against humanity, so I never got into the bar and club scene. I don't eat out often, preferring to cook my own meals so I can be sure of exactly what's going into my body. People find this annoying. That's fine. I find watching people fuel their body with wine, cheese and French fries annoying. But it's more than that. Tarkyn told me his friends found me intimidating and arrogant. Well, it's not a crime to be confident, and jealousy is very unattractive.

However, when it comes to friends, I have persisted with my mothers' group. Not so much because of the women—they're okay—but because I love their children and the friendships they've formed with Frankie. I meet with the group every Tuesday, even if I don't have Frankie, because I know it's what's best for my girl.

Today's catch-up done, I wave goodbye to Charlotte as she drives away with her two adorable little ones in the back. Little ones that I wonder if she even deserves, sometimes. That's probably way too harsh but she wasn't even watching when Imogen fell off the slide. Too busy bitching and moaning with the other mums about sleep schedules and how useless their partners are. They have no idea how lucky they are to have their kids with them all the time, to have company at home, someone who loves them.

*Will I ever feel loved again?* I wonder, starting the short walk home. I thought I had found my person in Tarkyn but he had me fooled. Even as a child, I felt alone. I had no siblings and the weight of the world on my shoulders when Mum died. It was my job to be what my dad needed me to be, and what he needed was a distraction. A project. He couldn't save my mum: the stroke was unexpected and she never woke up. But he could save me—from everything. Illness, disease, poverty.

Every day we exercised. Every day we studied. I always had Dad's company but I still felt lonely. I know Dad did these things to protect me and that was his way of showing love, but I was alone.

My phone buzzes, snapping me out of my pity party. Incoming FaceTime call from Tarkyn. I accept the call and his face fills the screen. He's outside somewhere with lots of background noise.

'Hey, Frankie wanted to talk to you,' he says. He sounds unimpressed, as though this request from his daughter is highly inconvenient.

Frankie's face appears. 'Hi, Mummy.'

'Hi, sweetheart. What are you doing today?'

'Zoo. Zoo. Look, giraffe!'

Frankie looks away from the screen and points to her left. But her mention of the zoo has turned my insides to fire.

'Frankie, sweetie, can I see Daddy, please?'

Tarkyn's face reappears. 'What?'

'Take it off video.'

His face disappears and I put the phone to my ear.

'What's the problem this time, Sloane?'

'You know I wanted to be the one to take Frankie to the zoo for her first time. We've been talking about it for ages and you *know* that.'

'Yeah, well, Janie got some zoo passes from her parents and we weren't going to waste them.'

'*She's* there too?' My voice is ice.

'Of course she is.'

'The zoo was my thing, Tarkyn. Not yours and definitely not *hers*. I can't believe you'd do this to me.'

I hang up and tears prick at my eyes. It's just a trip to the zoo but I wanted to be the first to take her. I wanted to be there the first time she laid her eyes on her favourite animal—the giraffes. And since when does Tarkyn call whenever Frankie asks? He did that because he knew it'd hurt. *Bastard.*

When I get home, I throw on my running gear and head out again, hoping a long jog will calm me down. But instead of spending the hour focusing on my breathing and taking in the world as it passes by, my mind races, replaying images of Frankie at the zoo, of Janie's bonding day with Frankie yesterday. *How are they taking all this time off?*

By the time I get home, I feel worse.

I fire off a text to Tarkyn.

*You'll pay for this.*

I don't even know what it means and I immediately regret it. I don't need to give him more ammunition to use against me. But I've had enough.

\*\*\*

*Anyone free to meet this afternoon?*

I text the mothers' group on WhatsApp even though we only just parted ways an hour ago. They probably think I'm a loser calling on them again so soon. But I don't have anyone else, and right now, if I don't talk to someone I'll end up sending more stupid messages to Tarkyn.

*Sorry, taking the kids to my mum's house.*

Katya's quick reply feels like a double rejection. Not only is she not available but she's seeing her mum, something I desperately wish I could do.

*I can't today, sorry.*

Charlotte gives no reason but part of me wonders if it's because Katya has already said she can't make it. The two of them have always been close—they live near one another and their husbands are mates, too. I'd be lying if I said I wasn't envious. Well, sorry I don't have a husband to entertain your husband.

I check WhatsApp several times over the next half hour. We created the group back when we met. It's only the four of us in there now but if you scroll back to the early messages, it's a diary of exhausted first-time mothers navigating feeding and schedules and sleep and safety, all while trying to look like they're totally coping.

My phone pings again.

*I can't leave prison, aka my home, twice in a day. Come over for a coffee. Any time. I'll just be sitting here, slave to the energy thieves.*

I laugh. Iris, always so dramatic.

*Thanks. Be over soon.*

When I arrive at Iris's house, the door is unlocked. She'd sent me a private text telling me to come straight in. I find her in a rocking chair with a twin in each arm and an exasperated look on her face. Billy is sound asleep on the couch with a half-eaten sandwich in his hand.

'Welcome to the crazy house,' she whispers.

'Here, let me take one of the girls,' I say, approaching her.

Her eyes widen. 'Don't you dare,' she hisses.

I take a step back, a little shocked.

'The girls sleep with one eye open,' she explains. 'Any change to their current position, noise level, temperature, hell, probably even my heart rate, and they'll make you pay.'

'Got it. I'll make some coffee then.'

She makes a face as though I've just offered her a slice of heaven. I'm not sure how she's going to drink it, though. Do I find her a straw? An IV?

It turns out it's a non-issue because as soon as I flick on the kettle, Billy wakes up hysterical that he's squashed his sandwich, disturbing the twins and freeing Iris's hands.

I struggle to listen to Frankie cry and she's just one child; Iris barely bats an eyelid as the three of her kids scream for her attention. The noise makes my ears ring. A lack of available sperm in my life is not the only reason Frankie won't be getting a sibling. *This* is not my idea of fun.

While I scoop instant coffee into mugs, Iris makes Billy another sandwich, changes both girls' nappies and sets them up on the floor under a baby gym.

Guilt pricks my insides. In comparison to Iris, maybe my problems aren't that bad.

'We can catch up another time if you like,' I say, handing her a mug.

'What? Don't be ridiculous. There will never be a better time. Not in the next eighteen years, anyway.' She plonks her coffee on a side table and wipes Vegemite from Billy's hands before he can get any more of it on the couch. 'Is everything okay?'

I take a seat in an armchair, one that isn't covered in Vegemite or spew stains, and Iris sits on the floor next to the twins, pulling faces and cooing at them.

'Of course.' I lie because I suddenly feel as though I have no right to struggle.

'Sloane, come on. You asked to catch up just a few hours after seeing us and you willingly came here knowing you'd bear witness to *this*.' She gestures at the room around her, which is covered in toys, spew cloths, an empty bottle of formula, a soiled onesie and three mugs half-filled with coffee.

I sigh. 'Okay, fine. Tarkyn and Janie took Frankie to the zoo today.'

'And?' Her eyebrows knit together and I realise that probably doesn't make sense to someone who's in a happy marriage.

'And, that was supposed to be my thing with Frankie. She's never been to the zoo before and he knows I was planning to take her.'

Her face softens. 'Oh, honey.'

I blink back tears. I'm not going to cry over this.

'I imagine this is probably one of many experiences you've missed—and will miss,' Iris says.

*Um, this is not making me feel better.*

'But,' she continues, 'an experience with Tarkyn and Janie is going to be very different to an experience she has with her mum. Frankie adores you and when you're with her, there's no one else in the world. She feels that.'

Iris is right. Frankie is my whole world, but she has to share her dad with Janie. 'That's true,' I say.

'Of course it is. I am nothing if not wise. Oh, and really good at picking the murderer in a good whodunnit novel.'

I laugh. 'Thanks, Iris.'

The next hour with Iris and the kids flies and by the time I leave, I feel better. I'm not going to let Tarkyn and Janie upset me. They will never be able to change my relationship with Frankie, no matter how hard they try.

# Chapter 7

## Charlotte

We haven't even backed out of the driveway and Imogen screams from her car seat behind me. 'Mummy, stuck! Stuck!'

I roll my eyes. 'Yes, sweetheart. You are stuck. That's what the seatbelt is supposed to do.'

She tugs at the straps, making exaggerated grunting noises as she tries to pull them off. Her latest tantrum trigger is her car seat, specifically how tight I do up the straps. I turn around and pretend to pull the little lever that releases the straps.

'That's better, Mummy.'

I turn back and hope she doesn't see the smirk on my face. Little faker.

The park is busy. Kids walk and ride to school. Dogs chase tennis balls. Men and women in corporate suits shuffle to the station.

Imogen battles with me to put on her helmet before giving in, letting me clip the strap under her chin and riding away on her trike. Jordy sucks on his dummy in the pram. He'll be asleep in minutes—such a champ at fitting into our busy toddler schedule. As usual, trains pass and Imogen shrieks. And as usual, I nervously peep into the pram to make sure Jordy hasn't been startled. His eyes are just rolling back now, lids closing.

We're coming around the bend at the top of the park where there's a main road and a cafe on the other side. When Imogen was a baby, I could cross over and get a coffee easily. Now I find it far too stressful with Imogen on her trike while I juggle a hot drink and the pram.

'Slow down, Immy,' I call to her.

She plants her feet and they skid across the gravel, bringing her to a stop. She grins back at me. An angelic grin that says, *See, I always do what I'm told.*

*If only.*

'Well, aren't you a good listener?'

I look just beyond Imogen and spot the woman who helped me at the car the other day. Imogen giggles and nods her head with enthusiasm. This kid could charm the grumpiest of Grinches with her giggle.

'Hey!' the woman says, waving at me.

I can't help but feel self-conscious in my oversized T-shirt as I take in her tight activewear and flat stomach that's on display again. I'm not fat by any means. I wouldn't be considered big at all, I don't think. But I don't feel myself. My name is still Charlotte, I still have hazel eyes and frizzy auburn hair, but it's like I've taken up residence in a new body. One I barely recognise.

'Hi,' I say, raking a hand through my unwashed strands. Her dark hair is again tied up in a pony, accentuating her soft features and high cheekbones. She's undeniably beautiful.

'Hair like Moana, Mummy,' Imogen says, looking up at her.

'Oh, thank you,' the woman says. 'I wonder if I could sail like her.' She pretends to swing around the magical oar.

Imogen squeals, clapping her hands. I didn't expect the woman to be a *Moana* fan. I figured her kids were older given her apparent freedom to run so frequently.

I smile at the woman, grateful to her for making Imogen giggle. It really is the best sound in the world. 'I'm Charlotte,' I say. I motion to the pram. 'Jordy's asleep and this is—'

She cuts me off. 'Imogen, right?'

My mouth opens in surprise.

'You mentioned her the other day when you were getting in the car. I remember it because it's just beautiful,' she says as she crouches down in front of Imogen. She puts out a hand for Imogen to shake, an adult gesture that Imogen finds downright hilarious. 'I'm Michelle.'

I nod, remembering my little mishap in oversharing the other day.

'So, I'm new to the area,' Michelle says. 'I haven't met many people yet. I hear the coffee over the road is pretty good. Do you want to get one?'

It's quite forward. Or maybe it's not. I'm not great at meeting new people or making small talk. But I can't imagine being in a new place with no one to talk to, so I feel for her. Plus, Imogen is smitten.

'Sure,' I say. 'We can walk and talk.'

Michelle smiles. 'Imogen, why don't I carry your bike while we cross the road?'

*Good luck with that*, I think. Getting Imogen off her trike is like removing playdough from a shaggy rug. Impossible. I know from experience of both.

'Okay, Moana,' Imogen says and I almost gasp. A burning sensation ignites in the pit of my stomach when I hear my daughter obeying this stranger when she rarely listens to me.

'Immy, her name is Michelle,' I snap.

'That's okay. I quite like Moana.' She winks at Imogen.

At the coffee shop we place our orders to take away.

'Cino, Mummy?' Imogen says in her sweetest voice.

I give her the standard mum look with my eyebrows raised and my head tilted to one side. She gets it.

'Please, Mummy.'

'You have such lovely manners,' Michelle gushes.

I roll my eyes because, let's face it, that please was forced. I add a babycino to our order.

Michelle carries Imogen's trike in one hand and her coffee in the other. Imogen grips her babycino in front of her with two hands as though it's the most precious thing she's ever held. And to a two-year-old, what's more precious than a cup of frothy milk and chocolate powder?

I discover that I have very little arm strength as I try to steer the pram with one hand and avoid spilling my coffee in the other.

The pram has a cup holder. A feature that I thought was the be-all and end-all when I bought it. Every mum needs coffee nearby at all times, right? Then I saw this horror clip on Facebook where a parent pushing a pram hits a bump on the footpath and the coffee tips and scalds the sleeping baby. Now I just deal with one-handed steering and hope that Jordy doesn't wake from the wild ride.

We cross the road and begin our lap of the park. It takes Imogen only a minute to grow bored of her babycino. Precious items only remain precious for fleeting moments in the world of a toddler. Her drink ends up in the cup holder—I figure a miniature cup of luke-warm froth is pretty safe. She takes her trike from Michelle and speeds off down the path ahead.

'She's really good at that, hey?' Michelle says.

'I think she'd ride it all day given the opportunity.'

Jordy starts to stir and we both instinctively peer inside the pram. His chubby little hand rubs at his face, the way it does when he tries to settle himself.

'Is he wearing a bracelet?' Michelle asks.

'It's a medical band. Peanut allergy.'

I was devastated when we learned he was allergic to peanuts. It was the first allergen we gave him when he started solids recently. The reaction was mild but we were told that it would likely progress to anaphylaxis. We're still in the process of getting into a specialist but for now he has this bracelet to remind us and everyone else that he can't have peanuts. I didn't think the bracelet was necessary given the only people who feed him are myself and Emmett, but Emmett insisted. His paramedicine background has made him so paranoid about this kind of thing. I'm not going to argue with him. He has Jordy's best interests at heart, even if Jordy does hit himself in the head regularly with the slightly too-big silver chain.

'Aww, poor bub,' Michelle says. 'That must be stressful.'

'Incredibly,' I say, trying not to picture the path ahead of us navigating childcare, school lunches and birthday parties. Any time I allow myself to think of leaving him alone with other people and food, my heart nearly stops.

'So, you said you were new to the area. Did you just move to Rosewood?' I ask, ready to change the subject.

'Yeah. A few weeks ago. Needed a change.'

'Where did you move from?'

'Lakesfield.'

The town sounds familiar but I can't pinpoint why.

'It's near the beach,' she adds.

'Nice. Can't believe you'd leave the beach for boring suburbia.'

She hesitates for a moment. 'My husband and I separated.' She pauses again. 'Our daughter spends a week with him and a week with me. But I couldn't stand to be in that town anymore.'

'I'm sorry about you and your husband.' *And the custody arrangement,* I think. It reminds me of Sloane's predicament.

'Oh, don't be,' she says, waving a hand in front of her. 'I'm fine. We didn't agree about things to do with our daughter. It's for the best.'

I sigh. 'Seriously, isn't that one of the biggest reasons couples argue?' I say. 'Disagreements over parenting. They don't show you that one in the movies.'

'So true,' Michelle says. 'Are you married, then?'

'Yep. Five years this year. Emmett's pretty great for the most part, but he thinks I'm a little soft sometimes.' I shake my head. 'He says I always make him the bad cop but I'm dealing with these two all day, every day. I have to pick my battles.'

I'm surprised how quickly I've opened up. I don't like to talk about Emmett negatively because he truly is a wonderful partner and father, but Michelle makes me feel so at ease.

'Absolutely.' Michelle's voice has a hard edge to it. 'You disagree now about parenting styles and one day it'll be about ...' She says nothing for a long time. I begin to think she's not going to finish. 'About your child's wellbeing or their future.'

I don't know how to respond to Michelle. She's clearly holding onto a fair bit of anger or frustration about her ex but I don't particularly want to hear about all the doom and gloom that awaits Emmett and I. Surely parents don't disagree constantly about everything. Emmett and I have similar views and morals, we'll be fine. I hope.

'How old is your daughter?' I ask.

'Three.'

I almost spit out my coffee, instead covering it up with a cough. I assumed she was much older, especially when she said her and her husband fought over their child's future.

'Sorry,' I say. 'Went down the wrong way.'

For a long, awkward moment, no one speaks.

Imogen breaks the silence, tumbling from her trike. It's a slow-motion kind of fall where she basically catches herself on the ground but it looks bad because her trike is on top of her. It happens daily but she still cries out, and because I am just *so soft*, I always pick her up and kiss whichever body part needs kissing better. I'll never stop doing that for my kids. *Thank you very much, Emmett.*

However, on this occasion Michelle beats me to Imogen's tangled little body.

'Aw, sweetheart. Are you okay?' she asks her.

I don't like the sound of someone else calling my baby girl sweetheart. She's *my* sweetheart.

'Sore finger,' Imogen says. Her tears have already stopped and she's on her feet.

'Let me have a look.' Michelle takes Imogen's hand in hers and pretends to inspect the damage.

I cross my arms. It's like Sloane at the playground all over again. 'She's fine. Back on your bike, Immy.' If only Emmett could hear me now.

'But, Mummy. Kiss better?'

Before I can even take a step towards Imogen, Michelle kisses her finger. My stomach lurches. This woman is practically a stranger and she's just kissed my kid's sore finger. That's definitely not okay. She could have who-knows-what disease. She could be sick. She could have something on her lips that irritates Imogen's skin. My mind is racing as I pick Imogen up and put her on my hip. I bring her hand to my lips and make a long, exaggerated smooching sound as though I'm trying to clean away the stranger's kiss at the same time as planting my own.

Imogen giggles. 'All better.'

'Sorry,' Michelle says, her face flushing. 'I didn't even think. Just reminded me so much of my daughter. She loves it when I kiss it better.'

'It's fine,' I lie. I hate confrontation. Soft with adults and my own children, it seems.

The conversation lulls a bit after that. We discuss the heatwave and which of the local cafes does the best coffee.

'What does your husband do?' Michelle asks as we near my car at the other end of the park. The same place where she helped me with the pram only a few days ago.

I find the question slightly odd given she hasn't even asked about my own job.

'He's a paramedic.'

She stops. 'What?'

I bring the pram to a stop next to her. 'You know, drives an ambulance, responds to emergencies.'

She shakes her head. 'Yes, I know what a paramedic is. It's just that … Never mind.'

We start walking again. Michelle is silent and I'm relieved when we reach the car.

As I put my bag in the boot, I remember the enrolment form. 'Hey, you didn't happen to accidentally take that Rosewood ELC form the other day, did you?'

Michelle glances away for a moment. It's only a split second but the movement unsettles me.

'No. I kept running laps after that so I wouldn't have been holding anything.'

I shrug. 'It'll show up, I guess.'

I bribe Imogen with chocolate to get her off her trike. Apparently my hair does not resemble Moana's enough to be obeyed. I wrestle her into the car seat where she is once again 'stuck' and she shrieks like the world is ending. Jordy wakes as I transfer him into the car and he begins wailing for food. It's a five-minute drive, he'll survive.

Michelle and I exchange numbers and say goodbye. She definitely overstepped with Imogen but I can't deny she's lovely.

I turn the key in the ignition and The Wiggles' 'Big Red Car' blares from the speakers, battling with Jordy's hungry cries and Immy's over-the-top screams.

It's a five-minute drive, I'll survive.

# Chapter 8

## Sloane

I'm walking out of an early morning spin class when my phone rings. It's Elka, my lawyer. This can't be good. I head to the changerooms and accept the call.

'Hello?'

'Sloane, I'm glad I caught you before work. Sorry it's so early.'

'That's okay. What's going on?'

'I'm afraid it's not good news. Our office received an email from Tarkyn's lawyers yesterday. He's applying for full custody of Frankie.'

The blood drains from my face and I lean against the lockers to keep myself upright.

'What?' I croak. 'How?'

'He says he has evidence of you threatening him and believes that Frankie will be better off in a two-parent family.'

'Well, he won't get away with it, will he?'

'Look, probably not. But you need to be careful with what you say to your ex and his partner. Don't give them anything they can hold against you. I'll make some calls today and let you know.'

I shake my head. 'Okay, thanks, Elka. Bye.'

I run my hands through my hair. I can't believe he's doing this. He can't take my daughter away. I grew her, she's a part of me. I grab my bag from my locker and take a shower. I'm tempted to call in sick to work but Tarkyn would probably find out and use that against me too. He'd call me unreliable.

When I arrive at work, I'm relieved to find that Jett has been discharged so I don't have to deal with him. That's one win on this extremely shitty day.

My first patient is Mrs Avery, a seventy-two-year-old woman who had hip surgery two weeks ago. She's a retired nurse with a major hero complex and behaves as though she's worthy of a war hero's care and compassion. The nurses can't stand her because she judges their every move. She begins each conversation with *Back in my day*, and inevitably ends it with an insult to their nursing skills.

'Good morning, Mrs Avery,' I say, striding into her room. I imagine flicking a little light switch in my brain that releases my ability to smile and empathise. It hurts, but I manage a slight upturn of my lips as she looks up from her crossword.

'Sloane,' she says. 'Those exercises you gave me are far too challenging. You can't possibly expect me to do those. Yesterday I spoke with your colleague and he gave me something more appropriate.'

My colleague—John. I work two days and he does the other three, and his favourite hobby is undermining me to our shared patients. Just another case of a man being intimidated and threatened by a successful woman.

'Did he, now. What did John suggest instead?'

Before she can respond, my phone shrills. The screen says Rosewood ELC. Frankie's childcare.

'Excuse me for a moment,' I say, holding up a finger. Mrs Avery glares at me as I step into the hallway.

'Sloane speaking.'

'Hi Sloane, it's Katie from Rosewood ELC. Sorry to call but Frankie's unwell. She's just started vomiting. Can you come and get her?'

'Oh. Um, is she okay?'

'She's fine, but you know we can't keep her here when she's vomiting.'

'Of course. Uh, so it's her dad's week. Have you called him?'

'We've left a message with Tarkyn but we need someone to get her as soon as possible.'

'Sure, leave it with me. I'll be there soon.'

*Argh.* I don't know what to do. This used to happen from time to time when Frankie first started childcare. The germs got her good. But Tarkyn hadn't returned to work permanently back then so I never got the calls. This is the first time I've had to leave early to go and get her.

My boss is a fifty-year-old divorcee who has no contact with his three children. He didn't take kindly to my falling pregnant, he wasn't happy that I returned to part-time hours only, and I am certain he won't be impressed with me leaving mid-shift to pick up my child. I was employed before he took charge of the physiotherapy department and since he was promoted, he hasn't hired a single woman under the age of forty. Most of the time, he doesn't hire women at all. Heaven forbid they have children.

I walk back to Mrs Avery's bed, pocketing my phone.

'I paid good money to have my hip repaired privately. That includes the after-care, you know.' Mrs Avery is scowling at me, disapproval all over her face.

'I'm sorry. It's my daughter—'

She cuts me off. 'Not my problem, love.'

*Is this old bat serious?* I desperately want to drag her little hospital table away so she can't reach her crossword, her water or morning tea.

I want to hang her buzzer and television remote just out of reach. But with that kind of bedside manner I'd probably be fired on the spot. And that would definitely be ammunition for Tarkyn and his damn lawyer.

Instead, I say, 'I'll be right back, Mrs Avery.' It's a lie but it's better than leaving her to piss the bed without a buzzer.

I pass my boss's office on the way out. I'm tempted to fake some tears but Leon's such a jerk, it'd probably make him angrier.

I knock on his door and pop my head in. 'Hey Leon, look, I have to head off. Family emergency. Sorry.' Then I walk away as fast as possible before he can ask any questions.

Despite the inconvenience, I'm excited to be seeing Frankie when it's not my week, even if she is sick. I wonder what's caused it. Tarkyn's probably been feeding her some disgusting pre-made children's meals filled with additives. Or maybe she had something bad at the zoo. The food stalls in those places are notoriously overpriced and drenched in bad oils and salt. I'll have to discuss it with him later.

I pull up at Rosewood ELC just as Janie comes out the front door carrying my daughter. Frankie's arms are wrapped around Janie's neck, her head resting on her shoulder. Janie is rubbing her back.

*What the hell?* Why didn't someone call to tell me they'd gotten on to Tarkyn? And why is the childcare centre releasing Frankie into the care of Janie? I didn't approve that.

'Frankie!' I yell from a few car spaces away.

Janie and Frankie both turn to look at me.

'Mummy!' Frankie says. 'Down, down.'

Janie puts her down and she runs into my arms. Janie follows behind.

'Sloane, what are you doing here?'

'What am *I* doing here? I'm here to pick up my sick daughter. What are *you* doing here?'

'The childcare centre called me. They couldn't get onto Tarkyn and they weren't sure if you were coming, so I left work.'

'Why would they call you?'

'I'm one of the emergency contacts, obviously. I'm on the list of people who can pick Frankie up.'

I shake my head. 'I don't think so. I remember filling out the form.'

'Tarkyn changed it. It didn't make sense not to have me, given I live with Frankie.'

I could kill him. First the email. Now the emergency contacts. He's cutting me out of Frankie's life. He's replacing me.

'Mummy, I want to go home.' Frankie's face is pale.

'Of course, let's get you home and we'll have a nice rest,' I say to her.

'Um, I don't think so,' Janie says. 'It's our week with Frankie. She's coming with me.'

I turn to Janie, ready to deliver a withering reply, and hesitate. Her expression has changed. Janie is usually plain. Timid. Boring. She's not attractive. She's not interesting. There are no features that stand out. But now, her face is fierce. Her dull brown eyes are alight with specks of yellow. Her cheeks have flushed, giving colour to her pale face, and her mouth is almost snarling.

But I don't get intimidated by women like Janie. I take a deep breath. 'It's *Tarkyn's* week with Frankie,' I correct her. 'He can pick her up from my place when he finishes work.'

'Sloane, I don't think you want to be breaching the custody arrangement. Especially with everything that's going on.' Her voice is low and sickly sweet.

I flinch. Is Janie the reason behind the email to my lawyer? Is she getting in Tarkyn's ear about this? I never expected things to get so nasty between us. Elka's words from this morning echo in my mind: *Don't give them anything they can hold against you.*

A lump forms in my throat but I won't let Janie see me upset.

'Frankie, sweetheart. Janie is going to take you home to Daddy and you can rest there.'

'No, no! I want Mummy.'

It's as though my heart is in a vice and someone is turning it, squeezing tighter and tighter until I can barely breathe.

'I know. But Daddy is going to look after you and make you feel much better, okay?'

Frankie starts to cry. How is a two-year-old expected to understand this? It's cruel.

I shoot a glare at Janie who watches us with a smug look on her face. Does she feel proud to be hurting a toddler like this?

I carry Frankie over to Janie's car and strap her in. 'I'll see you in a few days.' I kiss her forehead and turn to Janie. 'I'd like to know how she's feeling later, please.'

She nods, steps into her car and drives away.

I get into my own car and do something I haven't done in a long time. I cry.

# Chapter 9

## Charlotte

Katya was the first person I met at mothers' group. I was awkwardly trying to manoeuvre the pram into the Maternal and Child Health Centre and she held the door open for me, then I did the same for her. We bonded over it, at the time. Why do they make the doors to those places so heavy? How is a mother, recovering from childbirth, supposed to open a door and push a pram through, all the while trying not to accidentally bump the pram and harm her newborn child, who, at that stage, seems to be about as fragile as a butterfly's wing?

Katya and I sat next to each other that first session and went for coffee afterwards. It seemed like fate when we learned we lived a few streets away from one another. Now we catch up regularly in addition to our Tuesday mothers' group sessions.

After lunch and naps, I walk over to Katya's. Levi got a trampoline for Christmas so her place is the current favourite place to play in the eyes of Imogen and I'm more than happy to offload hosting duties. Katya is one of my best friends but I still feel as though my house has to look perfect when she, or anyone, comes over.

'Come in,' she says, as I park the pram at the front door. Imogen races through the house to the backyard and I take Jordy inside. 'Coffee?'

'No, thanks,' I say, thinking I'd much rather have a glass of wine. 'I've already had enough caffeine today.'

'So, have you heard any more from Sloane?' she asks, setting up a playmat on the grass in the backyard. She places Oscar on the mat with some toys and I put Jordy down with him. We drag some chairs from Katya's outdoor setting and sit next to them.

'No, only what she said in WhatsApp. Did Iris say anything?'

'Not to me,' Katya says.

I shrug. 'I'll check in with her later.'

Squeals of laughter ring out from the trampoline as Levi and Imogen bounce.

'How was your day?' Katya asks.

'Same old,' I respond. 'Although, I may have made a new friend.'

Katya gasps, clutching her chest. 'Are you cheating on me?'

I laugh. 'You'll always be my number one, don't worry.'

'So, who is she?'

'Her name is Michelle, she's new to town and has a daughter a similar age to Immy and Oscar.'

'You should invite her down to the park one Tuesday. The more the merrier.'

'Maybe,' I say. I hadn't even thought to ask her this morning.

Oscar's screams halt our conversation and Katya goes over to the trampoline before returning moments later, shaking her head.

'Those two,' she says, angling her head at the trampoline, 'switch between loving each other one moment and wanting to kill each other the next.'

'Sounds like a married couple,' I quip.

'Isn't that the dream?' Katya laughs. 'Anyway, how are you?'

I narrow my eyes at her. Don't I seem okay? 'Fine. Why?'

'I worry about you, Charlie.'

'Why are worrying about me?' I can't decide whether I'm offended or touched.

'I just know how much you've got on your plate. You know, with Jordy's allergy and Emmett's shift work. It can be hard.'

'I'm fine,' I say, indignant.

She drags her seat closer and takes my hands. It's weirdly intimate but at the same time it makes me want to burst into tears and pour all my worries out.

'Charlie, it's okay to not be okay.' I almost laugh at her use of the popular slogan. 'It's me. You don't have to keep it together around me.'

I swallow, trying really hard not to cry. I'm worried if I start, I'll never stop. I'm not a sad person. But how can I be fine if I don't even know who I am anymore? Sure, I could just tell Katya that life is hard because of Jordy's allergy and Emmett's work but that's not the whole truth.

The truth is, I'm riddled with self-doubt.

I miss my freedom.

I don't recognise myself in the mirror.

I don't recognise the person speaking when I open my mouth.

I'm an imposter in this unfamiliar body, trying to keep two children alive.

On cue, Imogen runs over, crying. She's bounced on her knees too many times and now they're covered in trampoline burns.

Saved by the wail.

# Chapter 10

## Sloane

'Sloane, don't be dramatic. I'm not trying to hurt you. I'm trying to do what's best for our daughter.'

Tarkyn is playing defence and I've got him cornered.

Despite Elka's advice this morning, I found myself dialling his number after dinner. *Just a quick check-in while I clean up the kitchen*, I told myself. I couldn't sit around all night waiting for news about my daughter that obviously wasn't going to come.

My voice is dangerously sweet. 'Frankie wanted to come with *me*, Tarkyn. She was hysterical. Do you really think that's what's best for her?'

'You shouldn't have been there.' He's practically whining now. 'If you hadn't shown up she would have been happy to go with Janie. Frankie needs the consistency of being in one place the whole week.'

My blood fizzes. It takes all my self-control not to absolutely let rip. He was the one who didn't answer the childcare call. How is that my fault? If I hadn't shown up, he'd attack me about that instead.

I take a deep breath and start stacking the dishwasher. Order always calms me. 'How is she feeling?'

'She's fine. Hasn't been sick since she came home, just tired.'

'Do you know what made her vomit?' Images of all the rubbish he's likely been feeding her race through my mind.

'Who knows? She's a kid. She probably caught it at childcare.'

I shake my head, grateful that he can't see my expression and report it to his lawyer. 'Well, make sure you only feed her bland food for the next few days. No dairy and absolutely no sugar. And make sure she only drinks water.'

I picture him rolling his eyes.

'I'm serious, Tarkyn,' I add.

'Yep. Okay.'

'Can I speak to her?'

'Janie's just putting her to bed.'

The fork I'm holding clatters to the floor. I try to take more deep breaths but this time I'm struggling to calm down. My cheeks burn.

'Is Janie the reason I got a call from my lawyer today?' *Oops. I went there.*

'Excuse me?' he says, his tone accusatory.

'We used to be happy. You loved me. I don't understand what's changed, how you could do this to me now.' I place another plate in the dishwasher, although I'd much rather throw it at a wall. 'But then today, it hit me. I don't think it's you. It's her. You're being manipulated, Tarkyn.'

'Sloane, this conversation is over.'

The line goes dead. I suppose I can expect another call from Elka.

I finish cleaning the kitchen and migrate to the couch. Usually, I like to meditate or read a book to wind down but I'm not in the mood for either. It's nights like these that I long for company.

I sigh and scroll to the Tinder app on my phone. I haven't used it in a while but sometimes the loneliness is overwhelming. Maybe some flirty banter will distract me from wanting to wring the necks of my ex and his girlfriend.

The first guy is wearing a muscle singlet, flexing hard. He's strong but his expression says he knows it and he loves it. No thanks. If I'm going to stoop to Tinder level, I need someone who worships my body, not their own.

The next guy is cute, in shorts and a T-shirt, no showboating. But he's holding a bottle of beer in a way that says 'drinking is life'.

When I turned eighteen and moved out of home, Dad was on his own. Without me around all the time, he no longer had a project to work on. I'd achieved everything he wanted me to: I'd been accepted into university to study physiotherapy so I would eventually have a good job; I'd saved enough money teaching swimming lessons to rent my own apartment; and I'd successfully completed a marathon, earned a black belt in jiu jitsu, and played in two university sporting teams.

Dad didn't cope well on his own. The first time I went home, he had made dinner. Healthy, of course, but then he offered me a glass of wine. My jaw dropped. I'd never had a drop of alcohol and as far as I knew, nor had my dad since Mum died. I declined and he drank on his own.

A few weeks later, I popped over during the day and he was watching the horse racing. It was only midday and there were three empty beer cans on the table next to him.

I was worried but Dad said he was just having a rough patch and would get help. I'd been so caught up in my studies and extra-curricular activities that I trusted he would.

I look more closely at the cute, beer-gripping guy, swipe left and throw my phone across the couch.

This is stupid. I don't know what I'm looking for or what I even want from a Tinder match. I need an app to find someone who'll just sit here and listen to me.

My thoughts go back to my dad. I've ended up alone, just like he did. He sought comfort in the bottle—maybe that's what I need, too.

# Chapter 11

## Charlotte

I've been putting off contacting Sloane.

It would have made sense to meet up with her when she reached out after mothers' group on Tuesday but Imogen had her swimming lesson. I wish I'd agreed to Katya's offer to chat to her this weekend at Parkrun. Now the guilt is eating away at me. Sloane definitely made a few sarcastic comments about Tarkyn at the last catch-up and I know now that's her way of asking for help. Sloane will never just tell us she's struggling. She's too proud. Tarkyn had been gone a month before she broke down one Tuesday and told us he'd left her.

Usually Imogen would be going to childcare today but she had a shocking night and I think she'll fall apart if I drop her off. Sometimes it's not worth the battle. My first thought is to suggest a play centre so Sloane and I can talk without being interrupted by the toddlers. But then I remember it's Tarkyn's week with Frankie so Sloane will be on her own. I'm tempted to drop Imogen at Katya's for an hour but Sloane would ask where she is and she already gets funny about how close my family is with Katya's. Finally, I settle on coffee, fire off a text to Sloane and load the nappy bag with snacks and entertainment.

Sloane meets me at the cafe, the same place I went to with Michelle. As soon as she walks in, I can't decide if this was a necessary conversation or a huge mistake. Usually, her stylish blond bob is tied half-up, half-down but today it's stuffed under a black cap, flyaways poking out from underneath. Her eyes are puffy and bloodshot and instead of fashionable activewear, she's wearing tracksuit pants and an oversized T-shirt that I can only guess used to belong to Tarkyn.

'Sloane,' I say as she slides into a seat between Imogen and Jordy's highchairs. 'Are you okay?'

'Yes,' she snaps. 'Why wouldn't I be?'

Her tone is aggressive and Imogen looks up from her colouring book, eyes wide.

'Sorry, of course I am.' She peers over at Imogen's book. 'What are you drawing, Immy?'

My hands clench into fists under the table. Hearing that pet name coming from Sloane's mouth makes my insides seize. I take a slow breath out and remind myself that my friend is having a hard time and, after all, it's just a nickname.

'It's a dog,' Imogen says, pointing to the scribble on her page.

'You are such a good drawer,' Sloane says and Imogen beams. 'So, what did you want to chat about? You said in your message you wanted to talk?'

My cheeks flush and I'm saved by the waitress arriving to take our drink orders. Why am I so nervous about checking in on a friend?

'Green tea, please,' Sloane says.

'I'll have a flat white and a babycino, thank you.'

The waitress is barely out of earshot when Sloane turns on me.

'A babycino? Really?' She arches a perfectly shaped eyebrow.

I know that look. It's the kind of look you get from strangers when you resort to bribing your screaming toddler with a chocolate bar.

'It's just a bit of frothy milk.'

'With chocolate on top. And probably a marshmallow.' She shakes her head. 'Do you know how much sugar that is for someone so young?'

I shrug. Most of the time, I eat the marshmallow anyway. 'It's just a babycino, Sloane.'

'And yet I'm the one receiving emails saying I'm not a fit parent and I don't deserve fifty-fifty custody. Frankie eats nothing but an organic, balanced diet and absolutely no refined sugar.'

*Did she just call me an unfit mother?* I swallow my outrage, telling myself it's just another one of her cries for help. Dammit, she can be a blunt bitch.

'What's going on? What emails?' I ask.

'Tarkyn's got his lawyers fighting for a change to our custody arrangement. He wants full-time care, so I'd only get to see Frankie on alternate weekends. Apparently, the way I live my life isn't appropriate for raising a child.'

*Woah.* For all her flaws, Sloane is a loving mother. I can't imagine what Tarkyn could be referring to.

'That's ridiculous. He won't get away with that. Frankie loves being with you, he couldn't do that to her.'

'I don't think he cares what Frankie wants. He just wants to be the perfect little family with Janie and Frankie.' Sloane blinks rapidly and fiddles with a napkin. 'Anyway, I don't know what I can do to prove myself. Being a single working mum is hard and even though I'm just doing what I need to do to get by, apparently that makes me a villain. A neglectful mother.'

I lean across to pat Sloane's hand. 'You have nothing to prove. And if you need any of us mums to write letters or references to support you, we will.'

She pulls her hand away. 'I don't think a written endorsement from someone like you would help.'

*Ouch.* What the hell is that supposed to mean?

'Excuse me?' I ask, my voice rising an octave.

'I wouldn't expect them to trust the word of a mother who feeds her toddler sugar, still hasn't gotten her son into an allergy specialist, and doesn't care about her kid at the playground. You weren't watching, Charlotte.'

For a moment, I can't breathe; it's as though she's punched me square in the gut. She's just taken my biggest fear, wrapped it up and shoved it down my throat.

'He's on the waiting list.' I'm not sure why this is the response I blurt out first. I don't need to be defensive about Jordy's allergies—I'm calling the specialists about openings daily and reading every article there is about peanut allergies. But for some reason it's what tumbles out. 'It's hard to get into a specialist. I'm doing everything I can.'

'Well, I would be doing more.'

The waitress arrives and I wonder if she can feel the tension as she quickly places our drinks on the table. Imogen's face lights up when she sees the babycino and she thanks the waitress in her sweet little voice. *See, my child has manners*, I think, desperately trying to convince myself that Sloane is wrong. *I'm a good mum.*

'Immy, sweetheart,' Sloane says, leaning over to my daughter. 'You don't have to drink that if you don't want to.'

Imogen looks at her as though she's just suggested trading in her babycino for a bowl of brussels sprouts and I'm proud that my girl's got my back.

'I want it.' Imogen looks at me, confused.

'It's okay, you can drink it,' I tell her.

'I can't watch this,' Sloane says, standing abruptly. She picks up her tea, walks to the counter, pays for something—I assume her own drink because I doubt she'd pay for mine or Imogen's poisonous cup of sugar. Then she pours her tea into a takeaway cup and leaves without another word.

'Well, that didn't go well,' I say, even though my kids have no idea what's going on.

Imogen just gazes at me, a milk moustache covering her upper lip, and smiles.

I call Katya on my way home and fill her in. She's as shocked as I am and frantically tries to think up excuses to get out of her run on the weekend.

'Maybe it's just me,' I suggest. 'Maybe Sloane is right—I'm just not a good mother.'

'Don't be ridiculous,' Katya says. 'You're an amazing mum. Sloane is clearly not thinking straight with everything that's happening.'

'I guess,' I say. But I'm not so sure. With just a few sharp comments, Sloane has unleashed all my insecurities.

At home, both kids go down for a nap—a minor miracle considering Imogen refuses most of her naps these days. Once they're asleep, I call the allergy specialist to see if there's any openings, and as usual, they regret to tell me that their next appointment is still several months away.

Then I take out my laptop and open trusty Google.

I type into the search bar: *How much sugar is in a babycino?*

Instantly, 176,000 results fill the screen. *Seriously. Maybe this is a bigger problem than I thought.*

I scroll past links to cafe websites and calorie-counting pages before clicking on an entry that tells me there is, on average, forty-nine calories in a babycino. That's less than both a banana and a mandarin, Imogen's favourite foods. I don't understand all the information about the different fats and sugars but I figure that a babycino every once in a while isn't going to induce type 2 diabetes in my toddler.

Sloane's biggest dig at me had been about Imogen falling off the play equipment while I was feeding Jordy. I had my back to the playground but we were sitting in a circle on our picnic rugs. I knew the other mums were keeping watch. I sigh. *I should've been more vigilant.*

I decide to search play centres around the area. I've only been to the same one a few times but I'm sure there are others. A confined space with lots of padded equipment, that's what I need.

I have a list of four play centres and three outdoor activities in the area before Imogen wakes from her nap. And I've almost managed to convince myself that I'm a dedicated, fun mum.

The feeling rarely lasts.

\*\*\*

In the afternoon, Emmett texts me to say he's invited our neighbour Bailey over for dinner. Usually this sort of last-minute plan would annoy me but I'm trying to let my 'cool, fun mum' vibe spill over into all aspects of my life, so I tell Emmett it's a great idea.

Bailey has lived next door for about a year now but it's only been in the last few months that we've really gotten to know him. Emmett loves him. Perhaps too much. It's a little cringey seeing an older dad try to act cool around a much younger, very attractive bachelor, but Bailey doesn't seem to mind.

Bailey arrives clutching a shopping bag and a bottle of wine.

'Grandma always says you should never arrive empty handed,' he says, passing me the bottle. 'Thanks so much for having me over.'

I smile. He's polite, good-looking and listens to his grandmother. How is he still single?

'And I got this for Imogen,' Bailey adds, pulling a doll out of the plastic bag. 'She had one out in the yard the other day and it got wet. Thought she could use a new one.'

'Oh, you really didn't need to. That's so kind.'

I usher him into the living area where Emmett is watching *The Wiggles* with the kids.

Bailey hands Imogen the doll and she squeals with excitement.

'Oh, hey, mate,' Emmett says, getting up to shake Bailey's hand. 'Sorry about this,' he gestures at the television. 'I'll turn it off.'

'No, don't be silly. I used to watch this when I was a kid.' He plonks himself down on the couch next to Imogen. 'Didn't two of them hook up?'

Emmett launches into a long, rambling story about which Wiggles got together, broke up, and who they're currently dating. Bailey nods, barely containing a smirk. When Emmett finally clocks that he's gone too deep, his face reddens and he clears his throat. 'Or something like that. Beer?'

I laugh quietly as I finish setting the table.

Emmett catches my chuckle as he passes me to get the drinks. 'Don't you start.'

'Maybe you can tell him about the Hi-5 scandal next,' I tease.

He rolls his eyes and heads back to the couch, beers in hand.

I grab my phone and order a few pizzas for dinner. Emmett told me earlier that Bailey had suggested Thai takeaway so he had to let him know about Jordy's peanut allergy—yet another reminder that we need to get that specialist appointment locked in.

When the food arrives, we all gather around the table, new doll included. I cut up Imogen's pizza because she prefers to eat it with a fork. In her world, getting pizza sauce on your hands is 'dirty' but playing with worms in the garden is fine.

'Feed me,' she demands, holding the fork out to Bailey.

'No, Imogen. You can feed yourself,' I say.

She's been doing this a lot lately. Now that Jordy is joining us for meals and needs to be spoon-fed, she wants to be spoon-fed too.

'It's okay, I don't mind,' Bailey says.

I know he's just trying to be a good guest, but it's frustrating. If Katya or Iris heard me say no to Imogen, they would back me. Bailey probably thinks he's helping.

'Here comes the aeroplane!' Bailey sings, flying the fork through the air before landing it in Imogen's mouth.

She claps. 'Again!'

I groan inwardly. We'll be doing aeroplane mouthfuls for the next month.

*Wait. No,* I remind myself. *I'm Charlotte, the cool, fun mum. This is great. My child is happy. It's all good.*

Emmett and I clear up the dishes while Bailey plays building blocks with the kids, defending his tall towers before Jordy or Immy inevitably knocks them down. He's a natural with children. If I hadn't seen him charming the other kids in the neighbourhood I wouldn't have picked it.

'Do you have kids in your family?' I ask.

He hesitates a moment. 'Nope.'

'You're great with them.'

He smiles. 'Thanks. How old is Imogen?'

'She's almost three.'

He nods, as though this means something important, before turning his attention back to the kids.

Once the kids are in bed, Bailey and Emmett go outside to sink a few more beers. I curl up on the couch and watch TV. I'm not really paying attention, though. I can't stop thinking about my morning with Sloane.

I text the group asking if they want to try out one of the new play centres I've researched tomorrow. Katya and Iris both have plans—appointments, family. Sloane doesn't reply.

When Emmett comes to bed, it's late but I'm still wide awake.

'Thought you'd be asleep,' he says, climbing in next to me.

'Rough day,' I say.

'Oh, Charlie. You should've said. I'd have kicked Bailey out hours ago.' He wraps his arms around me. We fit together perfectly, big spoon and little spoon. 'What happened?'

I twist around to face him. 'Just a run-in with Sloane. She made me feel so bad for giving Imogen a babycino and for not seeing her fall at the playground the other day. And she said I'm not doing enough for Jordy's allergies.'

Emmet laughs. 'Are you kidding me?'

I frown. He's not taking me seriously.

'Sorry,' he says, brushing some hair behind my ear. 'You know how protective I am of Jordy and Immy because I see so much horror at work. There is no one I trust more with our kids than you. You're an amazing mother and you're doing everything you can and more to keep them happy and safe.'

Tears well in my eyes and I bury my head in Emmett's chest. I press a muffled 'thank you' into his warm skin and he kisses me on the head.

# Chapter 12

## Sloane

I wake up Friday morning feeling like I've been hit by a bus. The custody battle, Wednesday's run-in with Janie and Tarkyn, my fight with Charlotte yesterday—I want to bury my head under the doona and wait for it all to pass. It's getting harder to remember why I live the way I do. Is there an easier way? A less lonely way? Or a way to forget the loneliness completely? Maybe Dad was onto something with the drinking.

Until this week I hadn't cried since I was in primary school and I lost the state cross country race by just a few seconds, but in the last two days I've cried more than enough tears to make up for it. My eyes are puffy and my head is pounding.

I can't do much about my predicament with Tarkyn at the moment but I can try and fix things with Charlotte. I owe her an apology. More than an apology. I know she struggles with self-doubt about her parenting so what do I go and do? Kick her while she's down, just to make myself feel better.

I contemplate buying her a coffee or sending some flowers but ultimately, I know the only thing that's going to work is what I have to say.

Half an hour in a hot shower makes me feel slightly more myself again. My eyes are less puffy and I can move my head without it throbbing. I complete my skincare routine because a lapse in my mood and emotions is no excuse to let myself go. Then I pull on a pair of denim shorts and a white crop and study myself in the mirror. That's better. I look strong, even if I feel tiny right now.

When I get to Charlotte's I hesitate on the doorstep before knocking. Footsteps thud down the hall, the door flings open and chaos erupts. Behind Charlotte I glimpse Imogen chasing one of the dogs with a toy golf club, shouting something unintelligible. Jordy is sitting in the highchair, screaming. The television is blasting some kind of high-pitched singalong program—something I'd never allow Frankie to watch.

'Sloane!' Charlotte says. 'Is everything okay?'

Charlotte looks flustered. Her hair is tied loosely on top of her head, her pyjamas—yes, *pyjamas*—are covered in what might be Weetbix, and she's holding a little container of puree. Chaos.

'Um, yeah, I just wanted to talk. Can I come in?'

She looks behind her. 'It's not a great time.'

'I know. But let me help.' I take the container from her hands and close the door behind me. 'Is this Jordy's lunch?'

She nods.

'Go and shower. I'll feed him.'

Her brows furrow. 'You really *do* think I'm a terrible mother, don't you. You think I need rescuing now, too?'

*Oh, damn.* This is not going the way I'd hoped.

'Not at all. I think you're an amazing mum who works so hard for her children, and you need a moment for yourself. Go and shower. Lock the door. Wash your hair. Stand there for a long time and do nothing.'

Charlotte is silent for a moment. I'm sure my offer is more than a little tempting. Eventually, she relents. 'Thank you.'

I shoo her away. When the sound from the shower comes through the wall, I turn off the television, sit down opposite Jordy and start spooning in mouthfuls of puree.

'Watch TV. Watch TV,' Imogen whines. 'Where's Mummy?'

'Hey, Immy. Mummy's in the shower. No more TV for now. Let's play some music instead.'

'Wiggles?' Her eyes light up and she drops the plastic golf club.

I hold back a groan. 'Sure.'

Imogen bounces up and down singing along to The Wiggles. When Jordy finishes his lunch I leave him in the highchair and he happily bangs his hands on the tray—his own version of dancing.

While the kids enjoy the music, I tidy the kitchen and make Charlotte something to eat. Judging by how flustered she looked, it'll probably be her first meal of the day. When she emerges from her room fifteen minutes later, hair washed and clothes clean, I place a plate of eggs and avocado on toast on the dining table.

'Sit,' I say.

'Sloane, what is all of this?'

'I came here to apologise. The things I said yesterday were awful. I took my anger at Tarkyn out on you.'

'You know, I googled the sugar content of babycinos? You made me feel terrible.'

I cringe. 'I know. That was so dumb. Of course, there's nothing wrong with an *occasional* babycino. And I know you're pushing for Jordy's appointment to be brought forward.'

Charlotte nods but she still looks hurt. 'Thanks for the food,' she says, digging into her eggs. 'And shower. I feel much better.'

'You're welcome. Anything else you need before I go?'

She shakes her head. 'You've done plenty. I'm taking the kids shopping shortly so at least I'm now organised for that. Thanks again, Sloane.'

I call goodbye to the kids, who are still bopping to the music, and let myself out, almost stepping straight onto a person crouching at the doorstep.

I yelp and a man with long, messy curls looks up at me. 'Sorry!' he says.

*Woah.* A white tee clings to the man's incredibly toned body and the muscles in his arms ripple as he places a large plastic container beside the door.

'No, all good,' I manage.

He stands up and grins. With dark blue eyes and golden curls, he looks like he's just walked off the set of *Home and Away*. He could pass for a bloody Hemsworth brother.

'Are you a friend of Charlotte's?' he asks, his eyes scanning my body. Now it's his turn to check me out. I don't think he realises that he's nodding his head. *Is that approval?*

'Yeah. Same mothers' group.' *Dammit.* Why did I say that? Revealing I have a kid is like flagging an STI. Guys tend to run away as fast as possible when they hear I'm a mum.

'You have kids?' He doesn't look disgusted or petrified. How refreshing.

'Uh-huh. A two-year-old daughter.' Then, in a hope to highlight my single status, I add, 'She's with her dad for the week. We share custody.'

He nods. 'I was just dropping off Charlotte's container. She made something for Mags the other day.'

'Mags?'

'She's our neighbour. She's about eighty. I live there'—he points next door then gestures across the road—'and Mags lives there. We all help her out with washing and cooking, odd jobs around the house, that sort of thing. I was just helping her prune the roses, actually. I probably stink.'

Whatever the smell is coming off him, it could easily be bottled and sold. I'm dizzy from it.

'Anyway, you didn't need my life story.' He laughs awkwardly.

Is he nervous? Am I making him nervous? All I heard is that he helps his elderly neighbour. He's hot. And he smells incredible. Is this guy real?

'I guess I better let you get back to it, then,' I say, smiling.

'Oh no, sorry. You're not holding me up. This is nice. Obviously.' He runs a hand through his curls. 'I'm sorry.'

'For?' I ask.

'For talking so much and being weird and nervous. It's just ... you're really beautiful.'

My heart races a little and my cheeks redden. 'Thanks.'

'I don't usually hit up women as they come out of my neighbours' houses, but do you want to get a drink this weekend?'

*Hell, yes.* 'Um,' I say, looking at my phone even though I know I've got nothing on. 'Yeah, that should work. Tomorrow?'

'Perfect. I'm Bailey, by the way.'

'Sloane. Nice to meet you, Bailey.'

We exchange numbers and he promises to call with details later.

'Well, I better get back to it,' he says, and winks. 'See you tomorrow, Sloane.'

# Chapter 13

## Charlotte

G rocery shopping with a toddler is like entering a parallel universe where your only goal is getting in and out in record time. However, your child is responsible for making sure that you end up buying additional, unnecessary items, engage in a public wrestling match over the trolley, and earn at least one side-eye from an elderly woman when your toddler licks the ground in protest.

Online grocery shopping and delivery has got to be one of the greatest gifts to parents. This week, however, a few items weren't delivered so a quick trip to the supermarket is necessary. I don't think I'd have made it without Sloane's help this morning. We'd probably still be in our pyjamas.

I score one of those pram parks near the entrance, although I have no intention of using my pram. The best way for me to keep Jordy safe as I chase Imogen around the aisles is to strap him to me in the carrier. Before kids I hated those pram spots taking up valuable car park real estate. Now I hate the people who arrogantly park their sports cars there.

Jordy's legs kick in delight as he watches the world go by from the carrier. When he was really small, he'd face me and fall asleep in seconds. Now he faces outwards and couldn't be happier with the view. He smiles at every stranger who goes by, and because weekdays at the supermarket seem to be reserved for parents or the elderly, I find myself having random conversations with the local seniors every week as they gush over the kids. Imogen holds my hand until we get to the trolley bay, then spends an age deciding which side of the trolley she'd like to sit in. Hopefully she actually stays there.

I grab the things that always run out before the weekly delivery: bread, milk and strawberries— Immy's favourite—plus the few items I couldn't get online. I sneak the berries into the trolley under the bread so she doesn't attempt to polish off the punnet before we even leave the store.

As I approach the checkout, Imogen's eyes light up.

'Moana!'

I assume she's spotted some toy or book that they put near the registers. The damn things are traps for parents.

'No, Immy. No treats today,' I say and she shakes her head and laughs.

'Hi, Imogen,' a voice says from behind.

I turn to see the woman from the park. *Moana hair*, I get it now.

'Hi, Charlotte. Hey, Jordy.' She tickles his feet, which are now kicking even harder.

I rack my brain for her name. 'Michelle, hi. Can't believe we keep running into each other.'

'I know, right?' She sounds like a ditsy teenager, a tone completely at odds with her usual cool mum vibe.

The checkout I'm waiting at clears and I do my standard cautious squat-and-lean movement to fetch the items from the trolley without bopping Jordy's head on the way down.

'Here, let me help,' Michelle says, grabbing an armload of groceries and placing them on the conveyor belt.

'Thanks,' I say. I'm a little embarrassed because I'm perfectly capable of doing the shopping on my own with the kids. I didn't ask for help. But, I must admit, I appreciate it. And the bigger Jordy gets, the more painful it is to lean over with him strapped onto me.

Michelle helps me load the bags back into the trolley and I tap my credit card to pay.

'Are you getting anything?' I ask, realising Michelle's hands are empty.

'Uh, no.' She hesitates. 'They didn't have what I was looking for.'

*The luxury of going to the shop for one item*, I think.

'So, do you work around here?' I ask, opening a packet of Tiny Teddy biscuits for Imogen.

'Haven't found a job yet.' She smiles. 'Hopefully something comes up soon.'

Outside the supermarket, near a small table and chairs, someone is dressed up as Bluey—Immy's favourite cartoon character. *Please don't see it. Please don't see it.*

'Mummy. It's Bluey! It's Bluey!'

*Shit.*

'Yes, sweetie. Would you like to get out and say hello?' I ask, hoping but knowing she absolutely won't say no.

Imogen launches herself from the trolley seat into Michelle's waiting arms. I wonder if she'd consider being my grocery shopping assistant every week—there's a job for her. Imogen runs up to Bluey and receives an enthusiastic high-five. A man, who seems to be escorting Bluey, bends down to say hello to her. He has grey hair and a short beard. His smile is kind but his eyes, which hold Imogen's gaze a touch too long, make me uncomfortable.

'Come on, Immy,' I say, keen to get away from Bluey's creepy helper.

'Drawing,' she responds.

'We have a Bluey colouring competition,' the grey-haired man explains. 'The kids are welcome to sit at the tables here and colour while you wait.'

'Maybe another time.'

'Please, Mummy.'

'I'm happy to sit with her if you have a few more things to do around the shopping centre,' Michelle offers.

I sigh. Once again, I soften. *Pick your battles.* 'Nah, it's fine. We'll stay.'

The man gives Imogen a piece of paper with a picture of Bluey and Bingo playing with a balloon. It's sad that I know exactly which episode it comes from. We've clearly watched too much *Bluey* recently. What would Sloane think? She'd switched off the TV as soon as I went into the shower this morning.

'The prize is a *Bluey* gift pack. There's one for each age group,' the man says.

I nod, trying to discourage conversation with the strange helper.

'When she's finished, just fill in the details and put it in Bluey's letterbox. We'll contact the winner next week.'

'Thanks.'

I'm not sure that you could say Imogen was colouring in. A more accurate description would be a dull squiggle. Perhaps 'Dull Squiggle' would make a good title for a piece of artwork one day. But today, it involves scribbling all over the picture of Bluey and Bingo using just one colour—brown. It's Imogen's favourite. The colour of mud and Vegemite, two of her most loved things.

'What a masterpiece,' I lie.

'It really is,' Michelle says. I'd almost forgotten she was here. She stands beside me, watching Imogen intently.

'Finished!' Imogen shouts. She holds up her drawing in front of her face and says, 'Beautiful.'

My girl certainly doesn't lack confidence.

I try to bend down at one of the tables to fill in Imogen's details but it's awkward with Jordy in the carrier. Plus, he's becoming increasingly agitated now that I've been standing still for a while—he wants to keep exploring the wondrous world that is the local shopping centre.

'I'll do it,' Michelle says. 'How old are you, munchkin?'

Imogen giggles but doesn't say anything. She has no idea how old she is.

'She's two,' I reply.

'Address?'

'Really?' I try to peer over Michelle's shoulder but she's blocking the page with her body.

'Maybe it's so they can post the prizes out,' she says.

I give my address and mobile number and Michelle copies it all down. Then she folds the paper in half a few times. Imogen acts as though all her Christmases have come at once when she gets to post her entry in the *Bluey* letterbox. It looks just like the one in the show. She pushes the paper through the slot and gives herself a big clap.

\*\*\*

By some miracle, Emmett finishes work on time and is home for dinner with the kids.

'I saw Bluey, Daddy,' Imogen says as he walks through the door. 'And Moana.'

Emmett smiles and looks at me. 'One of those days? Sounds like the TV was on a lot.'

I know he's not judging my parenting. We both use the television with Imogen on days where she doesn't nap and needs some quiet time or when she's driving us a little crazy. But still, I can't help but think of what Michelle said the other day and wonder if Emmett and I really are on the same page.

'No, Daddy. At the shops.'

His forehead creases and he turns to me again for clarification.

'We saw Bluey at the shops running a colouring competition and Moana is actually a woman called Michelle who has long dark hair.'

Emmett laughs.

'Moana is my best friend,' Imogen adds.

*I was her best friend yesterday*, I think. This woman carries her trike and compliments her scribbles and suddenly she's number one. I spend my entire day carrying things for her and boosting her ego. *Great running, nice dancing, I love your tower.* I shake my head. Why am I even bothered? She'll be best friends with a snail in the garden tomorrow.

I serve up dinner. Spaghetti bolognese and, for Jordy, some steamed vegetables. He quite enjoys mushing up the veggies in his hand before showing off his complete lack of hand–eye coordination while bringing the food up to his mouth. The two dogs hover below his highchair waiting for the scraps to drop. The vet has been lecturing me on the dogs' weight since Imogen started solids. Apparently a baby's table scraps is not a healthy diet. The dogs would beg to differ.

It takes less than two minutes for Imogen to be covered from head to toe in red sauce and pasta. I'm so glad Emmett is home early. Bathtime is going to be a messy necessity tonight.

Once the kids are bathed and in bed, Emmett pours me a glass of wine and we sit out on our back deck. The evenings are so balmy at the moment; pleasant temperatures spoiled only by the pesky mosquitoes.

When we're covered in bug spray, it's beautiful sitting out here in the early evening while it's still light.

'So, did you find the enrolment forms?' Emmett asks.

I take a big swig of wine and enjoy the way the silky, cold liquid feels going down. Since Jordy started sleeping through the night, this has become a bit of a habit. Now that I no longer need to get up and feed him, Emmett and I have been enjoying a few too many summer sundowners on the deck.

'No. But that Michelle woman—'

'Don't you mean Moana?' Emmett teases.

I roll my eyes. 'Yep, Moana, Michelle, whatever. She's the one who picked up the envelope for me the other day and she doesn't have it.'

'That's the same woman?'

'Yeah.' I purse my lips and run a hand through my hair. 'You know, it's weird. I've run into her four times recently. At the park and shops.'

'It's not that weird. I see the same people at the gym and the bottle shop all the time. You go to the same places, bound to happen.'

Being a regular at the bottle shop—that's a bad sign. But I suppose he's right. I do walk at the park during peak hour, before people start work and the weather warms up. Michelle probably gets her exercise in before starting her day. Although, what does she do all day with no kids or job?

'Are you creeped out or something?' Emmett asks.

I pause before answering because I'm not sure. I think about my conversations with Michelle. She seems lovely. Just another mum on a different parenting journey. 'No,' I say. 'But speaking of creepy, the guy escorting Bluey today was a total weirdo.'

Emmett laughs and then starts humming the *Bluey* theme song. It makes me chuckle too and for now I'm satisfied that we're on the same page, and we're doing a good job.

# Chapter 14

## Sloane

Every Saturday morning, rain, hail or shine, I do the local Parkrun. If I'm away, I find the nearest Parkrun and do that one. I walked the five-kilometre course the Saturday before Frankie was born, had her on the Sunday and was back on the course the following Saturday. It's a tradition my dad and I started ten years ago and I'm still going.

We used to run it together in those first few months after I left home. Then Dad's attendance became a little more sporadic and his excuses became increasingly flimsy, from car trouble to a bad night's sleep. I knew he was hungover. I always smelled the alcohol on him on the weeks he did make it.

Six years after I moved out of home, Dad died. It was slow, for him, anyway. He'd been diagnosed with liver failure years earlier but never told me. I guess he knew I'd move back in with him and make him my project. He told me before he died that he didn't want me to sacrifice the life I had created to be by his side.

The doctors advised him to stop drinking but he didn't—or couldn't. By the time I found out he was sick, it was too late. His skin was yellowing, he wasn't eating and he could barely move around the house on his own. I was so angry with him. Angry that he didn't tell me. Angry that he didn't try to help himself. Angry that he'd started drinking in the first place. And angry at myself for not noticing. I'd been so sure after everything with Mum that I could trust him to look after himself.

It was a Saturday morning when the hospital rang to tell me to come in. I'd just finished my run and rushed to his bedside. The last thing he said to me was that he was proud of the woman I'd become and that he was at peace leaving the world knowing I was strong, healthy and smart. Some days are harder than others, but that's what keeps me motivated. I've always prioritised my health for him.

This morning, Katya is joining me for Parkrun. I like being able to share my passion with people so when she mentioned at mothers' group one week that she wouldn't mind going for a run, I jumped at the chance to invite her. Even if it was a fleeting comment that she now regrets, I wasn't going to let her back out.

She meets me at the start line, dressed in activewear but somehow looking totally out of place.

'Sloane, I really don't know about this,' she says.

'You'll be fine. You can always walk if you need to.'

'*If*? You mean *when*. I can't run five kilometres. I haven't been for a run in years.'

I knew she was going to slow me down but I don't particularly want to walk the whole way. 'You might surprise yourself,' I say, for my sake as well as hers.

The crowd of runners gather at the start line and begin to move. Slowly at first, while we're all huddled up, then faster as people pull ahead. We take it easy to start.

'So, how are you?' Katya asks me and it feels loaded, as though there's more to her enquiry than polite conversation. I wonder what Charlotte has told her. Does she know about our argument at the cafe?

'I'm fine,' I say. It's not a total lie. Yes, I've cried a lot lately and I've been wallowing in memories of my father but I have a date tonight and I get Frankie back tomorrow. Things are looking up.

Katya's forehead creases. She's not buying it. 'How are things with Tarkyn?'

Now I know Charlotte must've blabbed. 'What about him?'

Katya's breathing is getting heavier as we slowly jog through the parklands. She bites her lip and between breaths says, 'Don't be mad.' Breath. 'Charlotte mentioned a call from your lawyer.'

Our pace is so slow that I could sing an aria without losing my breath, so filling her in is no issue. I give her the bare details about Tarkyn's attempt to get full custody of Frankie.

'That.' Breath. 'Must be tough,' she puffs out when I'm finished.

'It's fine. My lawyer says I have nothing to worry about.' Mostly true. 'Anyway, let's stop talking and pick up the pace.'

If Katya thought we were here to socialise, she had the wrong idea. She manages to run the entire way but we finish more than fifteen minutes behind my PB.

Katya beams when she crosses the finish line. 'I ran the whole way!' she says, doubling over and resting her hands on her knees.

No PB is fine. I did this to share what I love. 'And you'll get faster each week,' I reply, not even sweating, and can't help but hear my dad's voice echo through my own.

I wish he was here to help me. I'm sure a divorcee at risk of losing her child wasn't on his list of dreams for my future.

***

Bailey meets me at Brooke's Bar on Saturday night. It's a popular spot not far from Rosewood with a big garden out the back. I've been here a handful of times when forced to for an event of some sort and it's always busy on the weekend. I'm okay with busy. It gives me a feeling of anonymity.

We get a table out the back, in a corner. It's pretty private and a little quieter than other parts of the garden, which is nice, but we can still see and hear the band playing from where we are so there's less chance of awkward silences.

'What would you like to drink?' Bailey asks. God, he's good-looking. His eyes actually twinkle when he smiles.

'Um, I don't drink,' I say.

My thoughts drift back to my dad and a wave of sorrow crashes over me. One of the last times I saw him, he was still at home. I didn't even know he was sick then but I should've seen the signs. I'd popped in after work and he was slumped in his armchair, the cricket blaring from the television.

When I went to turn it down, his head snapped up and he yelled at me to leave it. There was so much venom in his tone that I dropped the remote control.

'Is everything okay, Dad?' I'd asked.

'Stop judging me and leave me alone. I was a mother and a father to you and then you left.'

He was drunk. I didn't visit him for months after that and the next time I saw him, he only had a short time left.

I'd been so angry and hurt after that visit. I had been everything he needed me to be and even though I knew it was the alcohol speaking, I couldn't help but feel like everything was my fault.

So, I'd left him alone. Now I'm alone.

'Sloane?'

Bailey's voice dissolves the memory and I turn my focus back to his attractive face.

'I was just asking if you wanted something else instead.'

I don't want to be alone anymore. I don't want to say no to every treat anymore. Or even one little drink. Time for me to stop being the person my dad expected me to be.

'Actually ...' I say, glancing at the drinks menu. It's like a foreign language; words like 'chardonnay' and 'shiraz' mean nothing to me. 'I'll have a vodka soda.' I vaguely remember a personal trainer saying once that if you must drink, that is a reasonably healthy option.

'You don't have to drink because I am,' Bailey says, and it's refreshing that he doesn't follow the Australian cultural norm of judging a non-drinker or accusing them of being pregnant or weird.

'No, no, I'm not. A drink would be great.'

He heads to the bar, his navy shirt hugging his broad, muscular back and shoulders. Bailey returns with my vodka soda and a beer for himself.

'Cheers,' Bailey says and I smile, clinking my glass to his.

I bring the glass to my lips, hesitating as the bubbles fizz around the bobbing ice. I only take a small sip, but it's enough for me to distinguish the vodka and the way it burns my throat. I can feel the liquid move from my mouth all the way down to my stomach, the sensation both unnerving and satisfying. I stifle a cough.

'You don't drink often, do you?' Bailey asks, making my cheeks flush.

'Every now and then,' I lie.

We engage in small talk between the band's sets. It's easy to talk to him and I learn that he enjoys exercise and runs his family's business. Before I know it, the band is packing up and Bailey's asking me back to his place for a nightcap.

I panic. I've nursed my drink all evening. I'm not sure I want another one.

He must sense my unease. 'Don't worry, I have tea, coffee or even just plain soda, although I do have vodka too.'

I relax. 'Sounds good.'

Whenever I tell the mothers' group mums about my dates with men and short-lived Tinder flings, they can't believe I manage it all sober. *How do you make small talk with them? How do you have the confidence to go back to their place? To have sex with a stranger?*

But I never feel nervous about dates or going home with guys. I only feel uneasy when I'm trying to figure out how to ditch them when I realise they're not what I want.

'You own this place?' I ask Bailey as he leads me through his house, past a home office and lounge room.

'Yep.'

'It's amazing,' I say, taking in a beautiful fireplace in the lounge. People rarely have real fireplaces anymore. There's something about tending to a fire that's calming and rewarding. Dad and I used to spend evenings by his old fireplace, reading or foam rolling, or both.

'Thanks.'

How does a guy in his twenties own a place like this in a suburb like Rosewood? It'd be worth close to a million, I reckon. It's absolutely stunning.

He stops in the kitchen and gestures for me to take a seat at the island bench—an enormous marble feature that feels more like a work of art than a place to prepare food. The kitchen is modern, with a fun, geometric tiled splashback and every appliance imaginable. His fridge even has a screen on the front of it, currently showing today's date.

Extremely attractive, helps out the neighbours, and rich. *He must be a serial killer*, I think wryly.

'What would you like?'

Feeling a little more invested in Bailey the more I get to know him, I let my guard down. 'Vodka soda again would be nice.'

He pours my drink before opening a beer for himself. Then we sit outside on his back deck on a comfy little outdoor sofa. The temperature has dropped since we left the bar and goosebumps prickle at my arms. I'm only wearing a tiny summer dress, I wasn't prepared for the cool change.

'Can I use the bathroom?' I ask.

'Just down the hallway on the right.'

Standing up, I feel the weight of my legs. I'm certainly more relaxed but I didn't expect this heavy sensation. I walk past the kitchen to the long hallway at the back of the house. There are several doors on the right. I open the first one and it seems to be his bedroom. There's an enormous king-size bed but, surprisingly, it's not decked out in standard bachelor dark colours. The quilt cover is cream and it's topped with cushions that seem to serve no other purpose than to be decorative. It looks beautiful, like something off a home renovation show. There are two doors opposite the bed, which I assume are the wardrobe and ensuite. I desperately want to snoop but I'm also desperate to get back to him.

The next door won't open. I twist the door handle a few times to make sure, but it's definitely locked. *Weird.*

'Bailey,' I call.

Footsteps approach and Bailey comes to my bladder's rescue.

'The bathroom's locked,' I say, pointing to the door.

'Oh,' he says, face reddening. 'That's my office. The bathroom is the next door along.'

I smile. 'Thanks. Be out in a minute.'

Walking back to the deck, I'm confused. I definitely noticed a home office at the front of the house when we came in. I remember because it was decked out with huge monitors and the most high-tech desk chair I've ever seen. Perhaps the back room is for storage for the office and the front one is just for show. People can get kind of weird about keeping up appearances in their homes. Maybe Bailey's like that.

I take a seat on the lounge and straighten out my legs so that they drape over his legs under the blanket.

'So, what motivated you to get into running and fitness?' Bailey asks me. At the bar earlier, I'd told him about how much I enjoyed exercising.

'My dad,' I say. 'Health was a big priority for him when my mum died.'

Bailey places a hand over mine and his touch sends tingles up my arm. 'I'm so sorry.'

'It's okay. It was a long time ago now. Dad was determined that I would grow up healthy and well-educated.'

'He sounds like a good guy.'

'He was, mostly.'

Bailey squeezes my hand but says nothing.

'I think I was just a distraction from him dealing with Mum's death because when I moved out, he fell apart. Like, really fell apart.'

I can't believe I'm telling him this. I barely know the guy. I haven't even told the mothers' group mums about my parents. I don't know if it's the vodka or the way he makes me feel, or both. There's something about Bailey that makes me comfortable. Like I could tell him anything and he would understand.

'Do you see him often?'

'He died of liver failure about four years ago.'

He looks down at the drink in my hand and then back at me, his eyes soft. 'You really didn't need to drink for my sake.'

I smile. 'I know.' I don't tell him that lately, loneliness has been pushing me to do things I never thought I would do.

'What about your parents? Do they live around here?'

Bailey takes a long swig of beer. 'Mum died when I was born.'

I suck in a breath, cursing myself for asking a stupid question. For assuming, just because he was younger, that his parents must be alive and well.

Before I can say anything, he continues. 'Dad and I got along well. I've always worked in the family business, but when he died last year, a lot of pressure fell on me. There were changes I wanted to make—still want to make—but I can't and I feel trapped. In many ways, he really let me down.'

I shift closer to him. We're more alike than I realised. Both of us are still struggling with demons from our past, demons from our fathers.

His hand finds my thigh and starts tracing lines up and down it, and I shiver. This time it's not the cold.

He pulls me closer so that I'm almost on his lap. I stare into his eyes and they are more than just the dark blue eyes of a young, attractive man. They are oceans, full of secrets and pain. The air around us grows thicker and all I can hear is the thumping of my pulse in my ears.

Bailey leans in, his mouth just an inch from mine. His hand moves to my cheek and he brushes his thumb over my lips. I sigh, still lost in his eyes.

Then he kisses me. At first it's soft, gentle. Then we can't get close enough to each other; we both need more, want more. He tears the blanket away and pulls me on top of him.

\*\*\*

At some stage during the night, we moved from the sofa to the bedroom. In the morning, I find my clothing strewn around the back deck. It was an incredible night. Bailey did not disappoint.

He offers to drive me home and as he backs his Range Rover out of the driveway, I pray that Charlotte isn't in the front yard to witness my exit, a thought made slightly worse by the tiny niggle of a headache. Two vodkas shouldn't warrant a hangover, should it?

Tarkyn's car is already outside my house when we pull up. Sometimes he calls before he leaves to bring Frankie home but he has a key so it doesn't really matter. Until now.

'Shit, shit, shit,' I say. I pull down the sun visor to check my face in the mirror. I'm in my outfit from last night and if my hair and make-up had a title, it'd be *Just Had Sex*.

'What's wrong?'

'That's my ex's car. He's already here with Frankie.' I rub under my eyes, trying to remove the mascara smudges. 'He's going to love this.'

'Why?'

'Long story.' I'd chosen not to share the custody battle with Bailey last night. I didn't want to scare him off with my divorce drama.

'Want me to come in?'

I look at him as though he just suggested I chop off a limb. 'Absolutely not. In fact, can you please drive a bit further down. I don't want him seeing you at all.'

'Sure,' he says, his voice clipped. I can tell he's hurt but I don't have time to explain or coddle him. I'm losing the battle for Frankie as it is. I don't need Tarkyn to add that I hook up with random guys and get home late on the days I'm meant to have Frankie.

Bailey doesn't look at me as I climb out of the car.

'I'll call you,' I say. He doesn't reply, just waits for me to close the door and drives away.

I walk up to the house, hoping I can just say I've been down to the shops. But Tarkyn knows me too well and he isn't going to buy the story that I've gone shopping in heels and a dress on a Sunday morning—especially if I don't have any shopping to show for it. *I'm screwed.*

'Where have you been?' Tarkyn says, opening the front door for me. 'And who was that dropping you off?'

So much for my incognito arrival. He must've been standing at the window watching the street. In fact, that's exactly the kind of thing he'd do. *Jerk.*

*Think, think, think.* Charlotte said she'd write something for me. Would she lie for me?

'I was at Charlotte's. She had a street party last night and I ended up staying at her place. The neighbour just dropped me home because Jordy was napping.'

I'll have to tell Charlotte everything now. But it's better than Tarkyn finding out the truth.

He scrunches his nose up at me, considering whether or not to believe my story.

'You look terrible. Go shower. Frankie's playing in her room.'

*How dare he?* Although, I know he's right. As I shower, I wonder what my night with Bailey will cost me. It's already cost me my sobriety, will it somehow cost me my daughter, too?

The night had been perfect. I've never been able to open up to someone like that. Even Tarkyn would struggle to find an issue with a man like Bailey. If I can accept, or more accurately, tolerate Janie, he will have to do the same.

# Chapter 15

## Charlotte

E mmett and I met in our first year at university. He was studying health science and I was in the journalism course. I always caught the bus to uni because I'd have to sell a kidney to be able to afford campus parking. However, one morning I snoozed my alarm too many times after a big night out and missed the bus. Usually that would be enough for me to justify ditching classes for the day but I had to submit an assignment, so I drove. When I returned to the car park after class, Emmett was standing at the ticket machine, running a hand through a dark blond mop. He looked up as I approached and gazed at me with the most beautiful green eyes I'd ever seen. My mouth must've dropped open but he didn't seem to notice.

'Sorry, my card isn't working and this stupid machine won't take my cash.' He was flustered. But even flustered, he looked good.

I don't know what I was thinking since I could barely afford my own parking but I offered to try my card and see if it worked. And it did. Next thing, I had coughed up two parking fees when I was meant to have caught the bus.

But like some kind of romance movie, it was all meant to be. Emmett insisted on taking me for a drink at the uni pub to thank me. We sat there talking for hours. A week later, my Facebook status was 'In a relationship'.

Emmett lived with his parents on one side of town and I lived with mine on the other. We would spend a few days at his and then a few days at mine. Our parents would get frustrated not knowing who was home or not home for dinner, or if they'd need an extra spot for guests.

It took years of working our butts off after uni to save a deposit for a house in Rosewood where Emmett grew up. And it was our dream home.

It's a five-minute drive to the park, train station and shopping centre but it feels as if we live in a quiet patch of countryside. Our two-storey home backs onto a reserve and from our deck we have 180-degree views of beautiful trees, home to native birds. The rosellas are my favourite. Imogen and I put out seed in a feeder for them every week.

Our house is at the bottom of a quiet, L-shaped court and our neighbours are lovely. We bring in each other's bins and collect the mail when someone goes on holiday. It's such a relief to be in a street where we always feel safe and always have someone to chat to.

This morning when I emerge with Jordy, Maggie is out watering her garden. She's the eldest resident in our court and we all look out for her. Her husband died last year and her kids are interstate so we've adopted her as our own family. She's often in the garden or slowly walking her dog up to the top of the street and back.

'Morning, Mags,' I call.

'Oh, good morning, dear. How's my favourite little family today?'

'Don't say that. The neighbours might be listening.' I laugh and so does she.

'You're not going to the park today?' she asks, aiming the hose at her perfect rose bushes.

'No, just a quick walk around here today.' To be completely honest, I just want to walk on my own with Jordy today. Between mothers' group and Michelle and Sloane, I need some alone time with my audiobook.

'Enjoy, dear.'

'Thanks. I'll pop over and do a load of washing later.'

She puts a hand to her chest in gratitude. The neighbours take turns helping Maggie with her washing, among other things. It seems to be the household chore that she just can't manage on her own, a fact we discovered last winter when she was doing the gardening in a summer dress, her teeth chattering as she made polite conversation.

I jam in my AirPods and hit play on my audiobook, a smutty college-sports romance. My guilty pleasure. At the top of the court, I turn right. To the left is the creek trail, which I avoid like the plague in summer because of the snakes. The right takes me towards the milk bar and primary school, where there are plenty of cars and people around to scare off any reptile friends that have slithered their way up from the creek.

A white SUV flies past me as I reach the end of my street, catching my attention. It slows down at the dead end and then stops completely. I keep walking in the opposite direction. People often park there to access the trail. Still, something doesn't feel right. I turn around after a minute or so and get a glimpse of the car. It hasn't parked, it's just idling there, brake lights glowing.

I continue my walk and before long I'm completely absorbed in the story—hot basketballer, hesitant college girl—so I don't hear the SUV coming up behind me, only see it as it crawls past. Guilt prods my chest—Emmett always warns me about wearing the AirPods while I'm walking, telling me about accidents he's been to where pedestrians wearing headphones have been hit by cars that they haven't heard. I try to see the driver but the windows are tinted dark and it speeds away. *Weird*.

I'm not quite so confident in myself anymore after two babies to assume that the driver was just checking me out in my activewear. But, maybe they were checking out the make of my pram. It's a pretty good one. Or maybe they were looking at Jordy. He's very cute when he sleeps. My mind turns over the list of maybes, trying to dull the rising worry.

When I reach the next intersection, the same car is parked up ahead on the left. Perhaps they're lost? I contemplate approaching the car to offer directions. But then I remember those horror stories you see on Facebook, where women are tricked into helping a stranger and before they know it, they're being sold to some creep in South America. I take a right. The school is up ahead and at this time of morning, there'll be plenty of foot traffic around.

I glance back and see the SUV do a U-turn and begin driving in my direction. I take out my AirPods, officially on edge now. My heart begins to race. I take deep breaths, trying to control the bubbling panic. As I walk, I contemplate my options. I can continue towards the school. There'll be lots of people and cars, but then what? Do I tell a random person that I think a car's following me? They'll think I'm crazy. Or, I can turn around and head home, but then if I *am* being followed the stalker will know where I live.

In the end, the idea of people, even if they think I've lost it, is more appealing than heading home to an empty house. I'm scared to look behind me. I don't want to know what the car is doing now. But, of course, I glance over my shoulder quickly. The car has pulled over again on the opposite side of the road. I increase my pace.

There's a steep incline up to reach the school. That, combined with pushing the pram, leaves me breathless when I reach the top. My panic settles slightly when the friendly face of the crossing supervisor, Reg, comes into view. He's worked at this school crossing since Emmett went to school here. He waves at every car that goes past and remembers the name of every student. He's basically a local legend, and today, my knight in high-vis armour.

'Morning, Reg,' I say.

'G'day love.' He peeps inside the pram and spies Jordy sound asleep, oblivious to my panic. 'What an angel. Where's Imogen today?'

'Childcare.'

'Lovely.' He walks to the middle of the road, holds up his stop sign and blows his whistle. 'Have a good one.'

As I cross, a car pulls to a screeching stop at Reg's sign. It's the same SUV. I freeze in the middle of the road, my pulse galloping.

In the brief moment that I stop, I take note of the car's number plate. I also sneak a glance through the windscreen. I'm almost certain now that this car is following me *and* that they don't want me to recognise them. The driver is leaning over to the passenger seat so all I can see is the back of a beanie-covered head and a puffer jacket. *In summer!* I can't even tell if it's a man or a woman.

'Everything okay, love?' Reg asks.

I wave at him and walk on. 'All good. See ya, Reg.'

When I get to the other side, I take out my phone and open the Notes app to save the registration number before I forget.

Reg walks back to his spot on the footpath, allowing the traffic to flow again. The SUV drives past the school and out of sight.

I collapse onto a bench seat and wait five minutes to be sure the car is really gone. Five minutes is a long time when you're scared. I scroll through Facebook. I do the daily Wordle. I even cull my emails, one of my pet hate jobs.

Finally, I set off towards home. Every sense is heightened. My ears prick at every approaching car, my eyes dart back and forth and my hands grip the pram so tightly my knuckles turn white. I'm almost back at the road that connects to our court when I hear it: the low purr of a car moving slowly behind me. It's the same car, *I know it*. I'm tempted to walk straight to the nearest front door and knock. But it's after nine. Most people have probably already gone to work. I pull out my phone and call Emmett instead.

He answers straight away.

'Babe, I think I'm being followed.' I slow to a snail's pace. I don't want this person to know where I live. Although, part of me is beginning to wonder if they already know.

I explain my morning walk to Emmett. I can tell he's worried by the tone of his voice but he stays calm.

'Have you called Mags or one of the other neighbours?'

'No.' *Why didn't I think of that?*

'Bailey usually works from home. Give him a buzz, he can jog up and meet you.'

'Okay, good idea,' I say. The car has pulled over again but its engine is still running.

As I search my contacts for Bailey's number, the SUV swings around and speeds away. I'm taking no chances. I get onto Bailey and within five minutes he's jogged to the top of the court and spots me just down the road.

'Thank you,' I say and burst into tears.

Bailey throws an arm around me and pats my back in an awkward, not-quite-a-hug embrace.

'Sorry,' I say, sniffling. 'I was just so scared.'

Bailey walks us back to the house. He even insists on checking all the rooms before we go in, which both terrifies and relieves me.

'All good here, mate,' he says. 'I need to get back but just call if anything else happens.'

'Thanks so much, Bailey.'

'Is Imogen at childcare?'

I nod.

'Do you want me to go get her?'

It's a sweet offer, but the last thing I need after a stressful morning is Imogen home early demanding snacks and cartoons. Still, it does give me an idea.

'No, that's okay. But, now you mention it, can I put you down as an emergency contact for her? It'd be so handy to have someone who works nearby.'

'Yeah, of course. Do I need to do anything?'

'Nope, I'll add your name to the list. It's Bailey McDonald right?'

He nods. 'What about a car seat?'

*Damn*. I'd forgotten about that technicality.

'Look, you'll probably never get a call, so don't worry about that.'

'Sure. By the way, I met your friend Sloane the other day.' He lets out a whistle as he exhales.

I raise my eyebrows. 'Did you just?'

'Yeah, we went out on Saturday night.'

My jaw drops. 'What?'

'Is that a problem?'

*Yes.* 'No. Not really. But she's just been through a nasty divorce and she has a kid.'

'I love kids.'

'You're young. Just be careful.'

I feel guilty for warning him off one of my friends but Sloane is so hot and cold and I know too well how harsh she can be when she's stressed or upset. I don't want Bailey getting hurt. I also don't want to be the middleman when it all goes wrong.

I thank Bailey again and lock the door behind him, checking it twice. So much for my quick walk and audiobook. Should've gone to the park.

# Chapter 16

## Sloane

Mondays on Frankie weeks are always a little bittersweet. I'm thrilled that she's with me again but I work Mondays. So on our first morning together, it's always a mad rush to get organised for childcare.

'I'll pick you up early today, sweetie. Mummy's only working until lunchtime.'

It appears my punishment for running out last week was to lose a few of my patients to John, so I have a free afternoon. I don't care, as long as Tarkyn doesn't find out. I'll tell him I took time off to bond with Frankie. Isn't that what we do now? Ditch work for all the bonding?

Frankie's face lights up. 'Then what?'

*Then what*. Frankie's current favourite phrase. She always needs to know what's happening next, and then after that, and then after that.

'And then we'll go and do something fun.'

'Then what?'

I shake my head and pull Frankie into a hug. 'Let's get to childcare, you cheeky thing.'

Childcare drop-off has always been really chilled with Frankie. I don't know whether to be proud, pleased or offended that she says goodbye to me at the door and runs off happily to greet her educators and friends. I don't envy the mums whose children cling to them like a koala, but a cuddle would be nice.

When I get to work it's almost nine-thirty. No time for coffee, then. My phone buzzes as I enter the hospital.

*Anything you need to tell me?*

A message from Charlotte, complete with a winking face emoji.

I reply with a single question mark and her response appears instantly.

*Maybe about a certain neighbour of mine?*

So, Bailey is the kiss-and-tell type. *Thanks, mate.* I check the time. My first patient isn't for another five minutes, so I call Charlotte. I need to word her up about Tarkyn anyway.

'Don't judge me. Your neighbour's hot,' I say when she picks up.

Charlotte laughs. 'He's also young, you cougar.'

'He's not that much younger than me.'

'I know, but you've been married. Don't give Tarkyn more things to hold against you.'

'Mmm. Yeah, speaking of Tarkyn ...'

'What's happened?'

'He saw Bailey drop me home yesterday. Talk about awkward.' I exhale loudly. 'Anyway, I told him I stayed at your place after a street party and that your neighbour dropped me home because you were busy.'

There's a pause.

'I'm sorry to drag you into it,' I add.

'Don't worry about it. I said I'd help with anything to do with the custody stuff. That's fine. If he asks, we had a great street party.' She chuckles.

'Thank you. Look, I've got to go, I'm at work. See you tomorrow?'

'See you then.'

I hang up and scan the notes on my first patient: Male. Seventy-eight years old. Broken collarbone. As I walk to his room, I fantasise about the elite athletes I should be working with. *One day, Sloane.*

***

When I pick up Frankie from childcare, she has food all over her face. Brown food. It looks suspiciously like chocolate.

'I'm taking Frankie early today,' I say to one of the teachers as I lift her onto my hip. 'What's all over your face, sweetie?'

Frankie grins.

'We had some cake to celebrate Dakota's birthday, didn't we, Frankie,' the teacher says in a sing-song voice.

*Cake?* I thought childcare centres were supposed to serve nutritious food. I didn't consent to cake.

'Sorry. What kind of cake?'

The teacher looks flustered. 'Oh, don't worry, it was egg, dairy and nut free and low sugar.'

'*Low* sugar? Do you have an ingredients list?'

There are toddlers arguing over a toy in the corner of the room and two others crying at the teacher's feet. I'd feel bad if I wasn't seething, *Why are you feeding my two-year-old cake?*

'I'm not certain, sorry, but I can have the chef write it down and I'll email it to you.'

'Great. Thanks.' I grab Frankie's bag. 'See you Wednesday.'

In the car, I shoot a text off to Tarkyn.

*Did you know they serve the kids cake at childcare?*

His reply pings straight away.

*Relax. A little cake won't hurt.*

Why did I even bother? I knew he wouldn't care. I'm sure Tarkyn feeds Frankie rubbish.

I pull out of the car park, still fuming, but I've organised something fun for Frankie so I force myself to forget it. At least for now.

We arrive at the local community centre and Frankie is bouncing with excitement. She has no idea why we're here but any outing thrills this kid.

I've signed her up to do a free trial of a kids' sports class. We can't come every Monday afternoon because I work but I figure if she likes it, we can come some weeks. It's important that she starts developing her coordination and understanding how her body moves.

I remember the first time Dad took me to the basketball court. I could barely throw the ball high enough to reach the net but we agreed that if the ball touched any part of the ring or backboard, I got two points. He had to get it in to get one point. We played one-on-one like that every week for years, each practice followed by a green smoothie at our local cafe. A treat. Some kids got ice cream, I got a protein-packed smoothie. As I got older and taller and stronger, the rules changed but the tradition never did.

'Hey, Frankie. Today we're going to play basketball. There'll be other kids too and you'll get to play together.'

She jumps up and down, clapping.

Inside the community centre, we make our way to the gymnasium. There are already a group of toddlers with their parents milling around. A young guy, probably no more than twenty, approaches us.

'Hey, I'm AJ. You must be Frankie. Welcome.'

He hands us a little name sticker for Frankie to wear and we follow him over to the rest of the group.

We sit in a circle and sing a welcome song with all the kids' names in it. Frankie cuddles into me—a little overwhelmed by all the people and the noise.

Next, AJ gets us to line up for some running races. I'm thrilled. I want Frankie to love this the way I do.

The first few races, Frankie insists I carry her. By the last race she's running, but I have to hold her hand.

'Don't worry. It always takes the kids a few weeks to warm up,' AJ says.

I wish I could bring her every week.

After the running races, we throw and bounce the basketball. Frankie has no interest in joining in. Instead, she holds her basketball like a baby, patting and shushing it.

I try to hide my frustration but I've never been the most patient person.

'Frankie, it's time to start throwing the ball,' I say a little too sharply.

She looks at me with intensity. 'Mummy, you can't throw a baby.'

I sigh. 'It's a basketball, honey, not a baby.'

Apparently that was the wrong thing to say, because Frankie runs to the side of the court with her 'baby' and cries. This is not going well.

The class finishes with an obstacle course, which includes balancing, shooting goals with the basketball, bouncing the ball and jumping. AJ plays music, which Frankie loves. She spends the entire time dancing in the middle of the course, basketball baby in her hands.

AJ smiles sympathetically. He probably thinks I'm a terrible mother who can't even get her daughter to focus on a basic coordination game.

It's disappointing, but I'll just have to work harder to find something active that Frankie enjoys. Maybe dance lessons. In my house, sport and fitness are non-negotiable.

For dinner, I roast some vegetables and toss them with quinoa.

Frankie scrunches up her nose. 'I want nuggets.'

'Not today.'

'Daddy gives nuggets.'

The joys of co-parenting. Good cop, bad cop. Good chef, bad chef.

'I'm sure he doesn't give you nuggets every night.'

She pauses, looking deep in thought.

'Where's meat?'

'I've told you before. We have meat-free Monday at my house. It's good for you and good for the planet.'

'What's the planet?'

*What have I started?*

'It's where we live. Now, eat up.'

She ponders my response and thankfully, it is satisfactory.

Frankie barely touches her dinner, though. Probably too full of cake. Which reminds me, I haven't received an email from the childcare yet. I'll have to call them tomorrow.

My favourite time of the day with Frankie is bedtime. We cuddle in bed and read stories until she falls asleep on me. I plant a kiss on the top of her head and sneak out, pausing at the door to watch her.

She looks so peaceful, so beautiful.

I can't lose her. I'll do whatever it takes.

\*\*\*

I'm sitting on the couch, updating patient notes on my laptop, when an email comes through from Tarkyn.

> *Frankie's teacher sent me this. I assume it's for you. Perhaps let Frankie enjoy herself, eat what she likes from time to time.*

Attached is the cake's ingredients list. Sugar. Butter. Cocoa. Frosting. If this is meant to be low sugar, what the hell are they serving at regular birthday parties these days?

But it's not the ingredients that upsets me the most, it's Tarkyn's words. To insinuate that I don't allow Frankie to enjoy herself is so ... *hurtful*. I enrolled her in sport lessons. That *is* fun, even if Frankie doesn't realise it yet.

A sudden urge to drink overwhelms me. *What is wrong with me?* There's no alcohol in the house and Frankie's asleep so I can't go out anywhere.

*Am I becoming my dad?* The thought shoots panic through my veins.

I close the laptop and take a shower to reset my spiralling thoughts. It takes a good fifteen minutes under the pressurised spray to convince myself that I'm fine. I'm just learning to relax and not take everything so seriously. That's a good thing, right?

# Chapter 17

## Charlotte

I drive slowly, carefully, to mothers' group. I've been on edge since my walk yesterday and now I'm constantly checking behind me, taking note of every car that passes. I'm not sure when I'll feel ready to take the kids for a walk on my own again.

I ended up going to the police station and reporting the incident. They said there wasn't a lot they could do—technically, no law was broken—and that some people just get a kick out of scaring people like that. However, they promised to look into the licence plate and told me to come back if anything else suspicious happens.

Emmett was furious when I told him.

'What about stalking? That's a crime.'

'I don't know. Maybe the car wasn't following me.'

'Charlotte!' He was so frustrated. 'You saw the car approach you and drive away, several times. It crawled up behind you. It stopped. They hid their face. It's not okay.'

We'd argued like that most of the evening. I was mad because I didn't need an angry husband that night. I needed a supportive husband who would hold me and let me finally breathe easy in his arms. But I knew he was only angry because he was scared. He was worried about me and the kids and he felt helpless.

So now, with little faith in the police, I triple-check every intersection and car on my way to the park. Even with the added safety of being
in my own car, I'm anxious.

It's an unseasonably cool day so when we arrive, I rug the kids up.

'No jacket,' Imogen yells and pushes the jacket away.

'Immy, it's cold. If you want to play at the park, you need a jacket.'

'No!' She snatches the jacket and throws it on the ground.

I run a hand through my hair, close my eyes and count to three. I
need to keep it together but what I really want to do is shout 'Yes!' and
force the jacket on her.

'Imogen,' I say. 'I know you don't like wearing your jacket but that's
what we have to do on cold days. Just like we wear a hat on hot days.'

She's good at wearing her hat—in fact, she loves it—so I'm hoping
this will resonate. Talking to a toddler is like defusing a bomb. If you
cut the right wire, say the exact right thing, you're sweet. But snip the
wrong one and your child will be flat on the ground, screaming and
kicking, while your plans are blown to smithereens.

Today I cut the right wire. Imogen's lips twist in understanding.

'Ohhh,' she says, as though I have opened her eyes to some unbe-
lievable new fact. 'Jacket on. Okay, Mummy.' She slides her arms into
the sleeves and runs off to play.

I sigh a breath of relief. One tantrum successfully avoided. When
will the next bomb need defusing?

I set up the blanket and place Jordy down. He rolls on to his stomach, grabs some grass and examines it, deeply fascinated.

The others soon arrive in a flurry of baby bags and prams.

'No Frankie?' I ask Sloane when she turns up alone. Frankie wasn't
here last week so this should be Sloane's week with her daughter.

Sloane scowls. 'It would appear not,' she says. Then her face softens. 'Sorry. That jerk insisted on taking her today and tonight because his parents are in town.'

'You okay?' Katya asks.

'Yeah. I just wanted her to play with the kids today. But it's fine.'

It was clearly not fine.

'Anyway,' Sloane continues. 'What's going on with you guys?'

We discuss toddler tantrums and the Target toy sale then I tell the group about the car incident and the police report.

'So, let me get this straight. The police aren't doing anything?' Iris asks. She's just finished giving a bottle to one of the twins and now the other one is stirring, ready for her turn.

I shrug. 'I don't think there's much they can do.'

Iris huffs. 'See, this shit just keeps happening. It's on the news every night. They do nothing and then the next time they're called, it's to identify a dead body.'

My eyes widen.

'Iris!' Katya snaps. 'No one is trying to kill Charlotte.'

My heart thumps. I can't believe this is our conversation.

'Are you sure they aren't doing anything?' Sloane asks, her voice wavering.

What else can I tell her? 'They said they'd look into the licence plate,' I offer.

'You must've been terrified,' Katya says. Her head swivels in the direction of the playground. 'Get down, Levi! You'll hurt yourself.' Levi has managed to climb on top of a piece of play equipment not designed for climbing. He gets down straight away. 'Well, that was a miracle. Sorry, Charlie, are you okay?'

'I was really scared but ... I don't know, maybe I had it wrong. Maybe they weren't following me.'

'Well, I'm only around the corner. Call if it happens again,' Sloane says, and the other mums add their 'me toos'.

'Thanks, guys,' I say. 'Okay, it's my shout for coffee this week. Usual for everyone?'

They all nod and I'm relieved Sloane doesn't offer to get the coffees. I want a moment to compose myself after Iris's dead body comment. As if my imagination needed that.

'Keep an eye on Imogen for me.' I pick up Jordy and cross the road, immediately regretting not bringing the pram. Usually I leave Jordy with the others but he's particularly clingy at the moment. I'll have to balance him on one hip and hold the tray of drinks in the other hand.

The cafe is humming with chatter, the clattering of spoons on saucers and the rhythmic hiss and clunk of the espresso machine. I bop a grizzly Jordy up and down while I wait for the order, losing myself in the familiar buzz.

'Charlotte!' the barista finally shouts.

I walk over, trying to game out how I'm going to manage this. I definitely overestimated myself.

Behind me, a familiar voice says, 'Here, let me take him.'

I turn to see Michelle smiling at me, her hands out. Perfect timing, again. I pass Jordy to her, waiting for his inevitable wail. It doesn't come.

'Thank you, thank you, you're a lifesaver,' I say, picking up the tray of coffees and shoving some sugar packets and plastic spoons into my bag. Michelle is now bopping Jordy, much the same way I was, except that now he's laughing. Typical.

'Um, did you want a coffee?' I ask, although I don't particularly want to wait any longer.

'Oh no, that's fine. I've just had one.'

'I just need to take these over to the park. I don't know what I was thinking, bringing Jordy. I need another arm or three!'

'I'll bring Jordy for you. Wouldn't want you spilling any of that liquid gold.'

I laugh. 'True.'

We make our way to the park.

'Where's your daughter?' I ask as we cross the road. 'It must be your week with her now, right?'

'No, not this week,' she replies matter-of-factly.

Strange, since I've been bumping into her for well over a week now and have never seen her with a child.

'My ex took her away for the week,' she adds.

Two weeks straight without her daughter, ouch. I'd be losing my mind.

Iris and Katya cheer when we arrive. Even Sloane looks keen for her long black. I hand out their coffees and introduce Michelle. Despite my hands being free and the blanket with plenty of toys on it, Michelle continues to hold Jordy, talking softly to him as if she's known him forever, when in fact, this is one of the few times she's seen him awake.

Katya gives me a knowing look. My lips pull downward on one side.

'Here,' I say, putting my hands out, 'I can take him now.'

'No, no, you relax,' Michelle replies, waving me off.

*What does that mean?* I *am* relaxed. Well, I was until now. Plus, it's strange for her to just hang around like this.

'I really should feed him,' I lie. I fed him just before I got coffee.

She passes him back, but not before pressing a little kiss to his forehead. There's a sharp inhale and I turn to see Katya's eyebrows raised. I hope Michelle doesn't notice, even though I feel exactly the way Katya looks. You don't kiss other people's babies. Not when you're basically a stranger.

'Anyway,' I say, hoping to encourage her to get back to whatever she was doing. 'Thanks for helping me deliver the goods. These mums need coffee!'

Michelle smiles. 'Any time.' But she still doesn't move.

'Moana!' Imogen's high-pitched squeal sounds behind me and I stifle a groan.

She bounds up to Michelle, jumping up and down.

'Oh hey, Lila,' Michelle says.

Imogen's face scrunches up. 'No.'

'I'm so sorry, *Imogen*.' Michelle whacks her palm on her forehead, her face reddening. 'You just remind me so much of my daughter.'

Imogen giggles and runs off to play again.

'Well, I'll leave you lovely ladies to it,' Michelle says, and stalks off towards the cafe.

'What the hell?' Katya hisses when she's out of earshot.

'I know. I know. She's a little odd. I met her in the park last week and now I keep running into her. She's new to town. Anyway, she's actually really nice.'

'Except for when she's kissing your kid or calling them the wrong name,' Katya says.

'Mmm, yeah. That's a bit weird,' I say. 'I didn't even know her daughter's name was Lila. It sounds familiar.'

Katya shrugs.

'It does, and she looks really familiar,' Iris says. 'I've definitely seen her before.'

'Probably around the park or shops,' I say.

Iris lifts an eyebrow. 'Charlie, I literally leave the house once a week, and that's to come here.' She laughs. 'The girls basically have me on house arrest.'

Even though she's laughing, I can tell she's hating these newborn days stuck at home. Our park morning must be the highlight of her week—the rest a blur of feeds, playtime and naps, most likely in front of twenty-four-seven news channels.

Later, driving home, the name Lila keeps bothering me. Why would Iris think it sounds familiar too? Has she bumped into Michelle before?

I really like Michelle, but every time I see her, I'm left with questions.

# Chapter 18

## Sloane

*I should be with Frankie, I should be with Frankie* circles around my head as I run on Tuesday afternoon.

Tarkyn and I have always tried to be flexible when it comes to special plans that fall on the other's week. But he asked me for this extra day before he hit me with a new custody battle—and that dig about Frankie needing consistency. I guess he thinks that doesn't apply to him. If I'd have known he was going to fight me for full-time care, I might have said no. But then again, I've always liked his parents.

They're a bit snobby, very proper, but I respect that they have expectations and a reputation to uphold. I wonder what they think of Plainey Janie. Tarkyn's mum would always compliment me on my outfits and figure, and she loved that I worked at the hospital. How would they react to my replacement, with her drab clothing and boring hair and make-up-free look? They weren't thrilled that Tarkyn ditched the family business (and fortune) to become a teacher so I know Janie's job won't impress them. I'd love to be a fly on the wall when they're all together. Definitely dysfunctional. Lucky, I suppose, that Frankie's there to break the awkward silences.

I'm meeting Bailey tonight—thought I'd make the most of having a night alone. He initially suggested we catch up on a night that Frankie's home but I shut that down quickly. We've been on one date; there's no way I'm ready to introduce him to my daughter. And especially not while I'm battling Tarkyn.

Frankie would no doubt tell her dad all about the lovely man who came to dinner and played with her and stayed until after bedtime, and Tarkyn would be on the phone to his lawyer in seconds. How dare I move on.

*Pizza and a movie at mine?*

Bailey's text arrives as I walk in the door and kick off my sneakers.

*Argh.* I'd forgotten how hard dating is when you eat healthily. Why do dates always involve alcohol and dessert or pizza and popcorn? But I really like Bailey. I don't want to put him off. Plus, I'm trying to be more carefree about this stuff.

*Sounds great. I'll bring a salad.*

He'll probably cringe when he reads that, but hey, baby steps.

I throw a jumper in my bag, along with a few overnight essentials. Presumptuous, perhaps, but I'm hopeful. Tarkyn is dropping Frankie at childcare in the morning so I'm safe from his prying eyes this time.

My stomach fizzes at the thought of seeing Bailey again. I don't think a man has made me feel like *that* ever, let alone three times in one night.

When I get to Bailey's, I park my car around the corner so that it's not sitting right out the front of Charlotte's house. I'm not in the mood for a lecture or a barrage of nosy questions about what we got up to. I walk quickly past her place and up Bailey's driveway.

When he answers the door he looks me up and down, taking in my tiny denim skirt and black singlet.

'Wow,' he says.

I smile. It never gets old, being complimented. That's why I don't understand why people like Janie make zero effort, or when other mums tell me about the block of chocolate they eat every night. It's hard work to look like this, but it's worth it.

I hand him the salad and he laughs, shaking his head.

'Of course,' he says. 'We can't have pizza without salad.'

I roll my eyes. He clearly has a good diet and exercise regimen—I've seen that body naked and it's perfection. But, he's young. He's probably still reaping the benefits of a fast metabolism.

I follow Bailey inside. This time I pay more attention to the home office at the front of the house. It looks pretty complete to me. There are shelves stacked with books and folders and a large filing cabinet, putting to rest my storage theory. Of course, there are the large computer monitors and fancy chair I saw the other day. There's also a giant map of Victoria with crosses and notes all over it.

'What's up?' Bailey says, turning around to me.

I've stopped in the hallway, staring at the office. I hadn't meant to draw attention to my snooping.

'Nothing,' I say, walking towards him. 'I'm just impressed. I do all of my patient notes on the laptop in my lounge room and you have *two* home offices.'

He squints his eyes and tilts his head. 'Huh?'

'That one.' I point behind me, where I'd just been standing. 'And the locked room down there.' I gesture to the back of the house.

'Ohh, right. Yeah.' He rubs at the light stubble on his jawline. 'That's just a junk room at the back. So I can keep my workspace at the front tidy.'

'Must be some valuable junk to be kept under lock and key.'

'Didn't know you were so interested in my junk.' He winks and I can't help but laugh.

During dinner, Bailey doesn't offer anything to drink besides water and I actually find myself feeling disappointed. He's probably not drinking because of what I told him about my dad. Little does he know I'm ready to let go. Yes, I'll bring a salad to pizza night. But I want to relax, let the walls down.

After dinner, he flicks through Netflix to choose a movie and I hatch a plan. Before Bailey can hit play on the thriller he's selected, I jump up and drag him to the kitchen.

'What's for dessert?' I ask playfully.

Bailey laughs. 'You paired lettuce with a margarita pizza and now you want dessert?'

'Yep.' I smile and run a hand slowly down his arm. 'And before you say it, I'm not talking about you.'

'And here I was about to cover myself in whipped cream,' he says.

'Tempting,' I say, and if it weren't for the excessive dairy, I'd jump at the chance to lick cream off every inch of his body. 'But what about a cocktail?'

His eyes widen. 'Sloane, you don't have to drink to impress me.'

'Please,' I say like a small child begging for a treat.

He opens a cupboard and pulls out a cocktail shaker. 'One Bailey Special, coming up.'

The cocktail is equal parts sickly in its sweetness and satisfying in the way it instantly warms my limbs.

We curl up together on the couch and Bailey starts the movie. My senses are heightened. The warm body beside me, pressing gently against my skin. The taste of gin and citrus and sugar lingering on my tongue. The sound of Bailey's breathing, as heavy and needy as my own.

I'm paying no attention to the movie with Bailey so close to me. I steal a look at him and he's staring straight ahead, jaw clenched. Specks of brown stubble cover his strong jawline and I lift my hand to trace a finger along it. His lips lift in a smile but he doesn't move.

I trail my finger down his neck, over his shoulder and to his chest. His breathing is visible, his pecs rising and falling beneath his tee. My hand continues down, over his abs that took my breath away when I saw them the other night. I stop above the waistband of his shorts, teasing him with tickling fingers that dip just below before coming back up.

Bailey's breath hitches and he turns to me, fire in his eyes. In one swift movement he picks me up and lays me on the couch, his knee parting my thighs. He lowers his lips to mine and I sigh as I dissolve into his kiss.

***

In the morning, Bailey makes me breakfast and a coffee. I don't start at the hospital until ten so it's nice to take it slow and be waited on. Is this how a relationship with him would be? I could get used to it.

As I'm packing my bag to leave, Bailey comes into the bedroom.

'Don't be mad,' he says.

I spin to face him. He's grinning, but his cheeks have flushed red.

'What is it?' I ask.

'I got Frankie something.'

'Oh.' I try to hide my shock. I can't give Frankie a gift from him. She doesn't even know he exists. 'That's really sweet. But you really shouldn't have.'

'I know. But I was at the shops yesterday and I wanted to get her a present.'

'Bailey,' I say, looking down at my hands. This is hard. I really like this guy. 'I'm not ready to tell Frankie about you yet.' I glance up again, dreading his reaction.

He shrugs and holds out a doll. 'That's okay. You told me about what Frankie was doing with the basketball on Monday and I thought she'd love it.'

I'd been texting Bailey the other night, offloading about the failed sports class and how Frankie thought the basketball was her baby. It's sweet that he remembered.

The doll is beautiful, with brown hair and a lifelike face. Definitely an upgrade from the cheap, tacky dolls she plays with at the moment. It's dressed in a green onesie and can move its arms and legs and turn its head. Frankie *will* love it.

'Just tell her you bought it,' he says.

I sigh. 'That's not fair, though.'

'One day, you can tell her the truth. I just want her to have it.'

*One day.* So there's a 'one day'. My stomach flutters.

I place the doll in my bag and pull him in for a kiss. 'Thank you,' I whisper.

# Chapter 19

## Charlotte

I wake up on Wednesday with a guilty conscience. Michelle went out of her way to help me deliver the coffee to the other mums and I didn't even invite her to hang out. In fact, I practically shooed her away, just because she was affectionate with my child. *Ugh*. I decide to apologise in person, get it off my chest. Plus, I want to know more about her daughter, Lila. Her name is *so* familiar. I text her.

*Coffee this morning?*

Michelle replies immediately.

*The same place as the other day?*

*Sounds good. The kids and I will be there at 9.*

When I get to the cafe, Michelle has already nabbed a table and set up two highchairs for the kids. I feel even worse knowing she's this thoughtful.

'Now, I've ordered you a flat white and Imogen a babycino,' she says as I organise the kids.

I shake my head. 'Seriously, you are too kind.' I slide into a chair and take a deep breath. 'And, I'm sorry about yesterday. You're new to town. I should've invited you to hang out with the group.'

'Oh, that's fine. I had things to do anyway.'

I can tell she's just trying to make me feel better.

'So, when does your daughter get back from her trip? She's welcome to join our Tuesday playground catch-ups.'

She says nothing for a moment and then glances at Imogen, who's already busy scribbling on some paper. 'Not using brown today, Imogen?'

Imogen looks at Michelle as if she's said something terrible. 'Brown is Jordy poo,' she declares.

I laugh, recalling that Imogen had helped me change Jordy's nappy this morning, only to discover that it was not a pleasant task.

Michelle laughs too when I explain, but her eyes don't quite match her smile. *Have I offended her?* She changed the subject as soon as I mentioned her daughter.

We chat for about half an hour and miraculously, the kids are perfect: Imogen colours in quietly and Jordy gnaws on a rusk. The poor little guy and his teeth. Michelle doesn't mention Lila once and I can't figure out a way to bring her up again without it being weird.

'I'll go pay the bill before these two realise they've behaved for too long,' I say.

Michelle reaches for her purse. 'You don't have to pay.'

'I want to. To say thanks.'

She smiles.

'Can you watch the kids for a second?'

'Of course.'

I go to the counter to pay the bill. It's been a nice catch-up but I still don't know Michelle any better than I did that first time we chatted in the park. A squeal pierces the cafe hum and I turn to see Jordy burst into tears. Michelle picks him up and starts shushing him. *It was only a matter of time.*

When the kids and I get home, we spend the rest of the morning in the front yard. It's shadier here than in the backyard at this time of day and it's already quite warm. The cooler weather didn't last long.

Imogen collects rocks from the garden and builds a pile of them, and Jordy sits on a picnic rug with a soft toy bunny. I sprawl out on the grass and gaze at Bailey's meticulous front lawn, recalling Sloane sneaking out his door this morning. I laughed when I saw her from my bedroom window. She was power walking up the street in a denim skirt and singlet, clearly not dressed for work. Another sleepover, then. I desperately want to text her, partly to warn her, and partly because I'm curious. I haven't been single in such a long time. I want to hear all the dating game goss. But I don't think she'd appreciate either type of text at the moment.

We're about to go inside for Jordy's nap when Bailey jogs over, carrying something brightly coloured in his hand.

'Here,' he says, handing me an orange rubber ring. 'It's a teether. Emmett said Jordy was teething pretty bad the other night when I was over. I thought I'd get him something to help. The woman working at the store said these are really good.'

I want to burst into tears at how thoughtful he is. 'Thank you, Bailey.' I hand the toy to Jordy, who immediately begins mouthing it. 'That's so kind.'

'No worries. I better get back to work,' he says.

We head inside. When I place Jordy down for his nap, he's really pale and limp. I knew he'd be tired from our outing but he doesn't usually just flop like this. His eyes are open, just. There are red spots around his mouth and his lips are swelling. Then it hits: he's having an allergic reaction.

My mind scrambles over the first-aid steps Emmett made me memorise. When Imogen started solids we went through choking, and when Jordy started recently, we went over it again. Then we found out about his peanut allergy and I think Emmett has officially drilled every fact about anaphylaxis into my head. The only problem is, we haven't had our appointment with the specialist yet, so we still don't have an EpiPen. In fact, the GP wasn't even certain we'd need one.

My heart pounds. I don't have time to call Emmett to confirm the symptoms and he'd kill me if I did.

I pick up Jordy, grab my phone and call an ambulance. My body is shaking but somehow it's functioning.

I put the phone on speaker and as soon as I tell the operator the situation, I shoot a text off to Emmett and another to Bailey. I'm shocked by my ability to remain somewhat calm. My voice is steady despite my heart racing.

I pace the hallway. Jordy vomits on my shoulder and I stroke his hair. 'It's going to be okay, baby.'

*Please. Please let it be okay.*

# Chapter 20

## Charlotte

'Send an ambulance,' I say.

The triple-zero operator peppers me with questions about Jordy's symptoms and I grow increasingly impatient.

'We just need an ambulance. Hurry!' I'm almost shouting now.

'Ma'am, an ambulance is on the way. Stay calm,' the operator responds, and continues to ask about symptoms.

It feels like time is standing still. Jordy's condition doesn't change and every time the operator asks how he is, I want to scream. Jordy's breathing is okay, but I know these things can progress quickly. Worse, I can't figure out why he's even having a reaction. *And where is this damn ambulance?*

Bailey knocks on the door and lets himself in. When I see him, the tears I've been holding back spill over. This time it isn't weird when he wraps his arms around me. His embrace is comforting and I sink into it, my heartrate slowly returning to a regular pace.

When Imogen hears Bailey's voice, she runs out of the room.

'Bay-wee!'

'Hey, sport,' he says.

'Immy,' I say softly, bending down so I'm at her eye level. 'Jordy's a bit sick and soon an ambulance will be here.' Her face drops but I can tell she's trying to be brave when she lifts her head high and nods. 'Bailey is going to stay here with you until Daddy gets home.'

'No, I coming.'

'Sweetheart, there might be lots of waiting around and I need to just focus on your brother for now.'

She shakes her head and my heart aches. Again, I find myself choosing one child over the other.

'Honey, someone needs to stay here to look after your baby,' I add, remembering the doll Bailey gave her. She's barely been without it since.

Tears well in her eyes and she wraps her arms around Jordy and I.

'Okay, Mummy.'

Bailey takes Imogen to the playroom.

Just as Jordy's breathing is getting noisy, the ambulance finally arrives. After a shot of adrenaline, Jordy improves significantly. He starts to cry and it's a welcome change from the quiet, limp little baby he was a few minutes ago. Emmett always tells me that crying is a good sign. The relief is overwhelming and tears stream down my cheeks.

'Any idea what he's reacted to?' one of the paramedics asks as she places an oxygen mask over Jordy's face. He tries to swat it away and screams but eventually his exhaustion gets the better of him and he lets it happen.

'No,' I say, patting my wet cheeks with my hand. I'm not exactly crying but I can't stop the tears from falling. 'He's allergic to peanuts. But he hasn't had any.'

'That's okay. We can investigate it further at the hospital. We need to take him there for observation and someone will speak to you about seeing an allergy specialist.'

I nod and silently curse myself for not pushing harder to get an earlier appointment with the one we're booked to see. 'Just let me say goodbye to my daughter.'

Imogen has Bailey wrapping up her doll in blankets. It's an adorable scene: young, buff guy playing dolls with a little girl. He should take a selfie for his Tinder profile. Although, maybe he's done with the apps for now.

'Be back soon, Immy. Thanks, Bailey.'

Imogen doesn't even look up from her doll. 'Bye, Mummy.' It's a good sign that she couldn't care less that I'm leaving. Bailey gives me a nod and I grab the nappy bag and go.

By the time we arrive at the hospital, Jordy is screaming for a feed. The paramedics help us get through the triage process at the emergency department and then set us up in a little cubicle so I can feed him. Doctors and nurses pop in often over the next hour to see how he's going and make sure he doesn't have a secondary reaction. I'm quizzed over and over about how Jordy may have come into contact with peanut, but I just don't know.

Emmett calls to check in. He left work early and is on his way home to Imogen. She's kept Bailey busy all afternoon, according to the photos he's sent through.

'So, you have no idea what caused it?' Emmett asks.

I almost scream. 'I have answered this question a hundred times. I don't know. I assume peanut.'

'Sorry. It's just, it's so scary, not knowing. Were you with him all morning?'

I exhale loudly. Is he accusing me of neglect now? 'Of course I was. We went to the cafe for coffee with Michelle and then played in the front yard.'

'Was he with you the whole time at the cafe?'

'Yes.' My grip on the phone is tight. I'm sick of being questioned. 'I was sitting with him the whole time, except when I ...'

'When you?'

I pause, thinking about the few minutes I left Jordy and Imogen alone with Michelle. She wouldn't have given him any food, surely. And she knows about his allergy.

'Charlotte.' Emmett raises his voice. 'When you *what*?'

'I went to pay the bill and Michelle held him when he got upset. It was only for a second.' Emmett goes to say something but I cut him off. 'Plus, we played at home for another half an hour after that. Don't these reactions happen instantly?'

'Usually, yes. But food allergens can take up to two hours to show symptoms. I've told you that.'

'Oh.'

'How well do you know this woman?'

'I don't know. Well enough that I wouldn't suspect her of sneakily feeding our seven-month-old a snack.'

Emmett is silent and my mind slips into defence mode. Here I am in hospital after calling an ambulance for our child who went into anaphylactic shock. Where the hell is my supportive husband? Why am I being guilt-tripped? Why do I feel like a terrible mother?

'I have her number,' I snap. 'I'll call her now.'

'Righto. Let me know when you have an update on Jordy.' He hangs up. I want to excuse his behaviour and say it's because it's been a scary day but I lived it too—more so—and I'm not being a jerk.

I find Michelle's number in my contacts. I've never called her before and I already feel nervous about the conversation. My palms are sweaty. Jordy is asleep in the hospital crib; I just need to do it. It's like ripping off a bandaid.

She answers after one ring. 'Hello?'

'Um, hey. It's Charlotte.' My voice is shaky.

'Is everything okay?'

'Not really. I'm at the hospital with Jordy. He had an anaphylactic reaction today.'

'Oh, my gosh,' Michelle says. 'Is he alright?'

'Yeah, he's fine now. It was pretty mild, I think.'

'Oh, thank goodness.' I hear her exhale. 'What caused it?'

'We don't know. We assume peanut. That's sort of why I'm calling.' I suck in air through my nose and try to calm the thumping in my chest. I hate confrontational conversations like this. 'Did you give anything to Jordy at the cafe today?'

'What? Of course not. He's a baby.' Her voice has gone up a notch and she speaks quickly. 'Why would you think that?'

'I don't. I just, well ...' I sigh. 'We don't know what caused it and that was the only time he was out of my sight, so I had to check. I'm sorry.'

I tense, waiting for the angry response. I'm accusing her of nearly killing my son, after all. My new friendship with this woman is over as fast as it started.

But the anger doesn't come.

'That's okay. It must be so stressful, not knowing. But I didn't give Jordy anything.'

'I didn't think so. Sorry I had to ask.'

'I understand.' She hesitates. 'Have you seen any of the mums from yesterday? One of them was eating a snack bar. One of those honey-and-nut protein ones. Maybe that did it.'

Sloane. She's always eating those bars, even though I've told all the mums, *no nuts around Jordy*. But she'd have been careful.

'I haven't seen Sloane today,' I say. Well, besides her quick exit this morning.

'What about eczema creams? Do you use any? Some of them contain peanut oil.'

'No,' I say, surprised by her knowledge.

'Is Imogen okay? Who's with her now?' Michelle asks abruptly.

'My neighbour—and Emmett will be home soon.'

'Right.' Is it just me or did her voice sharpen at the mention of my husband? 'Okay, well, let me know if you need help. I could do childcare drop-offs or pick-ups. Just say the word.'

'Thank you. And thanks again for understanding. I'll see you soon.'

I pick up Jordy and he doesn't stir. The poor thing, he must be so tired after his ordeal. I cuddle him to me and settle into the uncomfortable cubicle chair, stroking his fine blond hair.

'I'm not letting you out of my sight, sweetheart.'

# Chapter 21
## Sloane

Frankie's bubbling with stories when I pick her up from childcare. Apparently her grandparents bought her some new dresses. On the drive home, she tells me that they're 'only for at Daddy's'. I'm grateful that she can't see me roll my eyes.

'Well, I've got a little present for you, too.'

I hadn't planned to make a big deal of the doll from Bailey but the competitive part of me wants to one-up her experience at Tarkyn's.

'What, Mummy?'

'You'll have to wait until we get home.'

She bounces in her car seat and starts singing to herself.

It's funny how if you ask a toddler to pack up their toys, they forget after two seconds. If you ask them to brush their teeth before bed, they walk straight past the bathroom. But if you tell them there's a treat or a surprise or a present, that information is burned into their memory.

The second we walk in the door, Frankie politely asks for her present.

I sit down with her on her playmat and hand her the doll. She inspects it carefully, turning the doll over, running her fingers through its hair and straightening its clothes.

'I love her, Mummy. Thank you.'

'You're welcome, sweetheart.' And there's a stab of guilt in my chest because it's Bailey who deserves the credit.

While I cook dinner, Frankie looks after her new doll. She changes its clothes into something one of her other dolls was wearing. She puts a pretend nappy on it and feeds it a bottle. This kid is aching for a baby sibling. Poor thing is *not* going to get one from me. Nope. Sorry.

I shoot off a text to Bailey.

*The doll is a hit. Thank you.*

A minute later he pings a picture back. It's a photo of him playing dolls with Imogen. That's weird.

*What are you doing with Imogen?*

*Jordy had to go to hospital. I'm holding down the fort until Emmett gets home.*

*Jordy's in hospital?* I call Charlotte straight away.

'Hey, Sloane,' she answers, her voice tight.

'Hey. Bailey said Jordy's in hospital. Is he okay? What's going on?'

'Yeah, we're just going home now, actually. He had an anaphylactic reaction. Had to call an ambulance.'

I'm momentarily speechless. 'That must've been terrifying.'

'Very.'

'Sounds like Bailey is having a nice time with Imogen,' I say.

'Yeah, he's great with the kids.'

'Mmm. Why didn't you ask me to help? Is it because of our argument the other day?'

'No, of course not. You were at work and Bailey lives next door.'

'I really wish you'd called me,' I say. 'It seems strange to trust Imogen with a young guy when I've known her since she was born.'

Charlotte huffs into the phone. 'Sloane, seriously. Can we not do this right now? I've had a horrible day.'

'Right. Sorry. Just, remember I'm only around the corner.'

'Thanks. I'll talk to you later.'

I don't know why I'm so annoyed. Maybe part of me is jealous that Bailey is playing with Imogen and he hasn't met Frankie yet.

Later, when Frankie is asleep, I text Bailey again.

*I've been thinking about earlier, what I said about Frankie. I hope I didn't upset you.*

*I understand. Don't worry about it.*

Of course, he's understanding. But I want him to know how I feel. It's complicated with a kid. And I don't do feelings or emotions very well.

I type out a message and then delete the whole thing. I do this three more times before hitting send and throwing my phone across the couch. My cheeks burn.

Seconds later, my phone buzzes and I grab it. It's him.

*I really like you too. When you're ready for me to meet Frankie, I'll be there.*

Then he sends a photo of him in bed and my body heats. I wish I was there.

# Chapter 22

## Charlotte

Jordy is discharged from hospital late in the afternoon and we get home just in time for dinner. Imogen throws herself at us when I walk in holding Jordy.

I sit on the couch and Imogen wraps her arms around Jordy's head.

'Gentle, Immy,' I say and she loosens her grip around his neck.

'Jordy okay now?' she asks.

'He's just very tired. Did you have fun with Bailey and Daddy?'

'Yes, we make pizza.'

Emmett drops onto the couch next to us. 'We sure did. With extra, extra cheese.'

Imogen giggles.

'They're in the oven,' he adds. 'Shouldn't be too long.'

I smile. 'Thanks.' Then he puts his arm around me and pulls all three of us in for a hug. Tears spill down my cheeks and drip onto Imogen and Jordy's heads, but they're oblivious to my emotions because they're giggling at Emmett's bear growls.

'Bear hug! Bear hug!' Imogen cries with delight.

Emmett looks at me and brushes a tear from my cheek with his thumb. He mouths 'sorry' and I nod. We all say and do stupid things when we're scared.

We cuddle and tickle and laugh until the oven timer beeps and our hunger drags us from the bliss. The pizza is a little too cheesy in my opinion, but I don't say so. Imogen and Emmett are utterly thrilled with their efforts and compete to make the longest cheese string from their slice to their mouth. Imogen with her piece on a fork, of course.

I feed Jordy some mashed banana amid the chaos and even though I washed my hands thoroughly, carefully inspected the banana and sliced it directly into a clean bowl, I watch his every bite, monitoring his reaction. All the while Jordy watches his sister and dad, beaming as though they're putting on the greatest comedy skit of all time.

After the kids are in bed, Emmett goes to pour us a glass of wine and I decline.

'What if something else happens? We can't be drinking.'

He puts the bottle away without question. Maybe Jordy's hospital trip is the scare we needed to break the wine habit. Instead, we sit outside with a cup of tea, and Emmett has me run through the whole day again. He says it's so I can debrief and let out my emotions, but I still feel a little defensive as I take him through the day.

'Anyway, tomorrow afternoon we have to go back to the hospital to see a specialist. I don't think they'll be able to tell us what caused today's reaction but they'll be able to confirm the peanut allergy and give us a prescription for an EpiPen.'

'That's good. Ridiculous that it takes a serious reaction before you can finally get an appointment. The wait time is ridiculous.' Emmett takes a sip of his tea and scrunches up his face. 'And what did that Michelle woman say when you called?'

'She didn't give him anything,' I say, bristling. 'He was pretty moody all morning with his teeth—'

The thought hits me like a lightning bolt and I race inside. I find the teething ring on a table near the front door, where I'd left it this morning.

Emmett is right on my heels. 'What's wrong?'

'Bailey gave Jordy this teething ring just before his reaction. He was chewing it.'

'Why would it have peanut on it, though?'

'I don't know. Maybe Bailey had peanut butter toast and a trace got left on it.'

Emmett's face twists. 'Seems far-fetched. But put it in a sandwich bag and take it tomorrow. Maybe they can test it.'

I nod. We go back outside and my mind races over the what-ifs. *What if it had been more serious? What if the ambulance didn't come in time? What if the adrenaline shot hadn't worked?*

I massage my temples, trying to rub the thoughts away before they consume me. Jordy is fine. This time tomorrow, we'll have a plan and an EpiPen. He's going to be okay.

\*\*\*

Jordy's appointment was scheduled for three o'clock. At four-thirty, we still haven't been called in. I begin to call everyone I can think of to collect Imogen from childcare. Emmett is stuck at the hospital with a patient and at least an hour away. Bailey is in meetings. Katya has her hands full with her own kids. I hesitate for a moment and dial Sloane's number. She was so rude yesterday but she *is* great with Imogen.

'I'm sorry to do this, but Jordy and I are stuck waiting to see the specialist and I'm not going to get to childcare before close. Can you pick up Imogen for me?' I blurt as soon as she answers.

'Oh, shoot,' Sloane says. 'I've got Frankie and I only have one car seat. I'm sorry.'

Typical. Yesterday she cracked it at me for not asking her, and now when I need her she brushes me off. I bite my lip, telling myself her excuse is reasonable.

'Have you asked Bailey?' she asks.

'Yeah, he's held up in work meetings.'

'Okay, well, if you still haven't found anyone in half an hour, let me know.' She sighs. 'I'll call Tarkyn.'

'I'll keep making calls. Thanks, Sloane.'

I hang up the phone. I definitely don't want her to have to call Tarkyn. She'll hate that.

Against my better judgement, I call Michelle.

'Of course,' she says when I explain the situation. 'I'll get her and she can come back to my place.'

I know Emmett won't be happy having someone he hasn't met looking after Imogen but I don't know what else to do. I could be here for another hour and I might not make it before they close. Imogen will be beside herself with worry.

'Thank you so much. I'll phone the centre now and let them know you're picking her up today. Can you text me your address?'

'No worries.'

At that moment, my phone pings with a message from Bailey.

'Just a second, Michelle,' I say, swiping open the text.

*Meeting just wrapped—I can get Imogen. I'll be there by 5.*

Relief floods my body as I tap out a reply.

*You're a star! Thanks so much.*

'Everything okay?' Michelle asks.

'Yes, great, you're off the hook. Our neighbour, Bailey, is going to get Imogen. He's already on the list so it's best he does it. Thank you anyway.'

'Oh.'

She sounds disappointed, but I would really rather Bailey picks her up. And I know Emmett would too.

'Sorry to mess you around,' I say.

'Okay, I guess I'll see you soon then.'

Jordy begins to squirm in my arms. It's so frustrating when specialists run late like this. Especially when you have young kids. Jordy is overtired now so anything they try to do to him during his appointment will be a nightmare.

I'm just about to approach the receptionist to ask how much longer we'll need to wait when another text comes through. It's from Sloane.

*I've just dropped Frankie off at Tarkyn's. On my way to get Immy now.*

'Jordy! Jordy Jenkins?' booms a middle-aged man with a clipboard.

*Dammit.* I stand up and hurry over to him. I don't get a chance to reply to Sloane.

# Chapter 23

## Sloane

D ropping Frankie at Tarkyn's turns out to be even more awful than I anticipated. She doesn't usually have any issue going between us—we're lucky that she's always been able to adapt— but this afternoon, Frankie won't stop crying. She also has a firm grip on her new doll from Bailey. I asked her to leave it at my house because Tarkyn never lets Frankie bring dad-toys to my place so I don't see why I should share our stash. But, she clung to that doll for dear life when we left the house.

Tarkyn sends a text a minute after I drive away saying that the tears have stopped and Frankie is now happily playing with her doll. That makes me feel a little better.

When I get to the childcare centre, Imogen has already been collected. The receptionist tells me that she was picked up by a woman just five minutes earlier. I assume either Charlotte got away from her appointment in the end or perhaps Katya was able to go; the receptionist refuses to share any more details, despite Frankie going here and Charlotte knowing me.

On my way home, I call Bailey. The last few days have been so hectic and I want to vent. I'm pissed off that I ended up dropping Frankie at Tarkyn's for nothing. I need some light-heartedness. I know Bailey will deliver.

Charlotte mentioned he was caught up with work but I'm hoping to catch him at a good time. As soon as he answers, I know it isn't. There's a lot of background noise. Strange background noise. The sound of children: shrieks, cries, even.

'Hey, Sloane,' he says.

There's a bang and then the background noise is silenced.

'Hey. Where are you?'

'At work.'

'I can hear kids in the background. Are you moonlighting as a nanny?'

He laughs. 'Sorry. I *was* working. Now I'm with Imogen. Helping out Charlotte again.'

I must've misheard him. Imogen was picked up not long ago ... by a woman. The receptionist definitely said that much. 'You're with Imogen?'

'Yep, picked her up about half an hour ago.'

I cover my mouth, hoping he doesn't hear my sharp inhale. I pull the car over, rest my forehead on the steering wheel and try to slow my breathing.

'Sloane, are you still there?'

'Yep.' It comes out as a croak.

'Everything okay?'

I clear my throat. 'Yeah. Sorry, I've gotta go. Call you later.'

I end the call and squeeze my eyes closed. Why is he lying to me? And if that wasn't Imogen in the background, who was it?

Is he married? Does he have a secret family? Maybe that's why he's so good with kids.

I know there are a million possible explanations, but I feel sick.

# Chapter 24

## Charlotte

Jordy is prescribed an EpiPen and the doctor writes up an action plan. He makes another appointment with us for a test to determine what else, besides peanuts, Jordy could be allergic to. I wish he'd just do it now.

Before I leave, I mention the teething ring. The doctor says that it's rare but not unheard of that children sharing toys after eating certain foods can trigger a reaction. I explain that it was a gift from an adult and he's even less convinced that it could be the culprit. Nevertheless, he takes it and says he'll see if the lab will look at it but not to hold my breath.

On my way home I try calling Bailey to see how Imogen's pick-up went but there's no answer.

When I pull up at the house, it's swarming with police officers.

My heart races. *Something has happened to Emmett.* I hear all the time about paramedics being in accidents or attacked by drug users. I park the car and squeeze my eyes shut, hoping that when I open them the police will disappear like a bad dream.

Someone raps on the car window and I turn to see Emmett staring at me, a worried look on his face. I burst into tears. *Thank God.*

I get out of the car and he wraps his arms around me.

'What's happened?' I ask.

'Imogen's missing.' His voice breaks on her name.

'What?' My head spins and I drop to my knees. She's been at child-care and then with Bailey. How could she be missing? I press my palms into the cold concrete of the driveway and try to find the composure to speak.

Emmett meets me on the ground and takes my hands, dragging me up.

A car door opens and I watch, dazed, as Katya pulls Jordy out of his seat. I didn't even realise she was here. Her face is pale.

'Bailey went to get Imogen from childcare but she wasn't there,' Emmett is saying. His voice sounds distant.

'What do you mean, she wasn't there?'

'Someone else picked her up.'

'Sloane! I asked Sloane to do it,' I say. Relief explodes through me as I remember the text she sent that I never got a chance to reply to, as well as the several missed calls I hadn't returned during the chaos this afternoon. *It's just a big misunderstanding*, I think.

Katya speaks up. 'No, Sloane called me because she also went to the centre and was told Imogen had been collected. She thought I must have gotten her.'

'This isn't possible!' I'm almost yelling now. They don't just hand the kids over to anyone who asks. What the hell is going on? My chest tightens. I take out my phone and begin searching my contacts for the centre's number. My watch reads 6 p.m. They should still be there.

Emmett gently takes the phone from my hands. 'I've already spoken to them,' he says. 'So have the police.'

He runs a hand through his hair. It's trembling. I stare at him, waiting for answers.

'So, Eva was the room leader who signed Imogen out. She told me Bailey picked her up at about ten to five.'

'I thought Bailey said she was gone when he got there.'

'Yep,' he says. 'But she was adamant the name was Bailey.'

'Did she check ID?'

'No,' he continues. 'Eva said a woman arrived and introduced herself as Bailey. When Imogen saw her, she started calling her Moana.'

I cover my mouth with my hand. *Michelle.*

'The woman said to Eva that Imogen calls her Moana because of her hair and that she didn't have ID on her but that you'd asked her to pick up Imogen because you were held up at the hospital. They took Imogen's reaction as a sign it was the right person.'

'They took a two-year-old's excitement to see someone as a positive ID? Are they serious? Immy gets excited by anyone who walks, talks or looks in her direction.' I shake my head. How could they be so negligent? 'What happened when Bailey got there?'

'They freaked out, realised they'd made a mistake, and called me. Bailey had to get back to work—some sort of emergency. Anyway, isn't your new friend the one Immy calls Moana?'

'Yes, Michelle. I asked her to help out this afternoon, but Bailey got back to me when I was on the phone to her so I told her not to worry. Why would she pretend to be Bailey? I don't … I don't get it.'

My head swims. I grab my phone off Emmett and dial Michelle's number. *Please, God, tell me this is all some sort of silly mistake.*

The call doesn't connect. It doesn't even go to voicemail. 'She must have switched her phone off,' I say, looking wildly at Emmett.

I pace the driveway. Then I fall to my knees again and smack the concrete. It hurts like hell and I scream. But it's not just the pain in my now grazed hand, it's desperation, fear. How could the childcare centre be so careless? How could *I* be so careless? I howl into my hands and Emmett lifts me up again and pulls me into a hug.

'We're going to find her, Charlie.'

*\*\*\**

Soon after, the police ask us to go with them to the station to give a statement. I ask if Emmett can sit in with me but they say it's best for the investigation if we give our statements alone.

Katya takes Jordy for the night. I send him with strict instructions to give him no solid food and pack up a little bit of frozen breastmilk, but it won't be enough if he wakes through the night. Katya assures me that she has plenty of her own frozen breastmilk that she'll happily give him. It feels weird to think of him drinking someone else's milk but I'm not in a position to be picky.

I can't believe that I have to part with Jordy just twenty-four hours after calling him an ambulance. I feel like I'm being tested. Pulled in one direction by one child and then the other direction by the other child, and no matter what I do, I can't be enough for both.

All my fears are becoming reality. I'm not the mum I want to be. Before we decided to have kids, Emmett and I travelled and worked and lived an easy, safe life. We had responsibilities—jobs, pets, a mortgage—but we never worried about things. From the moment Imogen arrived, it started. The little voice in my head that says I'm not a good mum, I'm failing, I'm bad at this. Emmett tells me I'm too hard on myself but how can you accept anything but the best when it comes to your own children?

Driving away from Katya's house, away from Jordy, is one of the hardest things I've ever had to do.

I sit in the cold interview room at a table across from two empty chairs. There's a small window high up on one side of the room. Through the sheer white blind, I can just see the sun starting to go down. A woman in plain clothes comes in and sits opposite me.

'Mrs Jenkins, I'm Detective Kitchen. I'm sorry you're going through this. I'll be as quick as possible so we can get you home.'

I nod. She starts to fiddle with some electronic equipment connected to the wall beside us.

'I do need to record this conversation.' She struggles with a cord. 'Just a minute. There, got it.'

I suddenly feel like a suspect being interviewed. But I suppose it makes sense to record it. Then I won't have to repeat it over and over.

Detective Kitchen and I talk for almost an hour about how I met Michelle. She asks me if anything strange had happened recently. I almost forget the incident with the SUV following me until she asks me to walk her through each day in the last week. I tell her that I already reported that to the police, as Iris's words haunt me. *It's on the news every night. Dead body.*

Detective Kitchen nods and leaves the room. When she returns, she tells me that they've identified the driver of the white SUV but she doesn't say who it is.

Then I tell her about Jordy's allergic reaction.

'You say Michelle was the only person left alone with Jordy?'

My stomach lurches and I cover my mouth.

'You don't think that's related, do you?' I ask. 'She said she didn't give him anything.'

'It could be.'

I swallow back bile. I've been too busy to eat today so there's nothing to bring up. 'I don't understand.'

'Sometimes, kidnappers become fixated on their victim and will find ways to involve themselves with the family. They make you feel vulnerable. They may cause an incident, like a hospital visit where you're distracted by another child, exhausted, worried. They prey on your poor decision-making.'

I exhale sharply. That stings.

'I'm sorry, Mrs Jenkins. I didn't mean for it to come out like that.' The detective looks at the ceiling and sighs. 'But yes, it's possible that Jordy was targeted to distract you.'

I shake my head. I just can't believe someone would do that. And Michelle. She seemed so kind. A little in my face, maybe, but harmless. I drop my head into my hands and close my eyes. I try to think of all the times I saw her. The park was the first time, when she was running. Then again when she helped me get Jordy into the car.

'The enrolment forms,' I mumble.

'Sorry?'

'The enrolment forms for Imogen's kindergarten went missing. I actually asked Michelle if she had them because she picked them up the other day when they fell from my bag. She said she gave them back to me but I don't have them. I don't know if it matters, but I just thought of it.'

Detective Kitchen jots something down on her notepad. 'Anything else?'

Then it hits me. It hits me like a freight train and my whole body shakes. I grip the table in front of me. 'Oh,' I gasp.

Detective Kitchen looks up from her notepad. Her eyes are wide. 'What's wrong?'

I take a deep breath, trying to steady the shaking. My chest feels as though it's being crushed. 'She called Imogen by another name the other day, by accident. Lila.' Tears well in my eyes. Now I know why it sounded familiar. 'That's the name of the girl who went missing in Huntley last month.'

The detective's mouth forms a straight line and the crease between her eyebrows deepens. She nods. 'We believe the woman who took Imogen is Lila's mother, Amalia. Michelle matches her description and Amalia drives a white SUV with the registration number you reported.'

I don't know what to say. I don't know how to feel.

Michelle is Amalia. Michelle stalked me in her car to make me feel vulnerable, scared. Why me? Why Imogen?

Questions continue racing through my head.

Is it a good thing that Imogen is with another mother? Does that mean she's safe? Or will she punish Immy if she isn't a perfect replacement? I assume that's what this is. Some kind of sick replacement.

Detective Kitchen mutters a few things into the tape recorder before taking me out to Emmett.

We get in the car and I fill him in. Emmett seems relieved that they know about Amalia and her situation, but I don't share his optimism. She's clearly unhinged.

We drop past Katya's on the way home so I can feed Jordy. Emmett updates Katya and I take out my phone. The screen is filled with messages from friends and family. It seems Imogen's face is plastered on every news site and social media platform. Emmett updated our families while I was being interviewed so I lock my phone and ignore them all.

I really want to take Jordy home with us but I know it's better that he stays with Katya. We could get a call at any hour about Imogen and I don't want to have to worry about who's looking after him.

Before we leave, Katya tells me to call Iris but she doesn't say any more than that.

When we're back in the car, I call her.

'Hello,' Iris whispers. 'Hang on.' There's a muffling sound and then a door closes. 'Hey, sorry. Didn't want to wake the twins. Charlie, I'm so sorry about Imogen. They'll find her. I just know it. Gosh, you must be so worried. Well, we all are, of course. I was talking to—'

'Iris,' I say, cutting her off. She's rambling and I need answers. 'Katya said to call you. What's going on?'

'Well, when I was pregnant with Billy, I had shocking insomnia.'

I roll my eyes and look at Emmett in the driver's seat. He's watching the road but I can tell he's straining to listen. There better be a point to this story. I put the phone on speaker.

'I used to stay up all night watching late-night news,' she continues. 'There was a story in Lakesfield about a local man being murdered and half the mothers' group were interviewed about it.'

I vaguely remember the story. 'Yeah,' I say. 'And?'

'I became really obsessed with the story because I was pregnant and I knew I would eventually be in my own mothers' group. So I ended up Facebook stalking the mums.'

Of course she did. Iris loves news and current affairs and if there's a rabbit hole of information to fall down, she'll fall. Hard.

'One of the mums looks just like that girl, Michelle. I *knew* she looked familiar. Her actual name is—'

'Amalia.' I beat her to it.

'Yeah,' she says. 'Isn't that creepy? How did you find out her name?'

'The police told me. She has Imogen. She's also the same Amalia whose daughter went missing in Huntley last month.'

She gasps. 'Of *course*. I remember seeing her briefly on the news then too. Oh Charlie, I'm sorry it didn't click faster. I'm just so tired.'

'No,' I say. 'Don't apologise.'

'She won't hurt Imogen, she's a mother.'

'You don't know that, Iris,' I snap. I'm sick of people telling me it's okay, that Imogen won't be hurt. She's missing and nothing makes sense anymore.

Iris goes quiet and I release a long sigh. 'Sorry. I'll let you know if I hear anything.'

I hang up and Emmett and I drive in silence the rest of the way home.

There's a woman out there who's connected to a murder, who's recently lost her child, and tonight she has our daughter.

# Chapter 25

## Sloane

I'm home when I finally get through to Charlotte, and she's hysterical. Katya has already told me what happened. I was right: Bailey *had* been lying about picking up Imogen. But the actual situation was far worse than I could've imagined.

Imogen is missing.

Kidnapped.

By that woman who Charlotte introduced us to at the playground.

I *knew* she looked familiar. And I hated the way she spoke to Imogen that day. All sweet and playful like they'd known each other forever.

'What can I do to help?' I say to Charlotte on the phone.

'Nothing. None of us can do anything. It's hopeless.'

She sounds broken and of course, she would be. I can't imagine how she's feeling. It's hard not having Frankie with me every day but at least I know where she is and that she's safe.

I don't know what to say.

'Look, Sloane, I've got to go,' Charlotte says.

I hate myself for not knowing the right thing to say to comfort her.

'Okay, well, let me know if you hear anything or if you need anything.'

I hang up to find a text from Tarkyn.

*Frankie's had dinner. She's almost ready for bed. Is she staying here?*

My heart aches. This will be the second night this week he's had her during my time. But I need to be available to help.

*Imogen has been kidnapped. It's probably better that she stays with you so I can help out.*

*That's awful and I'm really sorry. However, you have interesting priorities, Sloane.*

His reply stings. I imagine him adding this to his growing list of reasons why I'm not fit to be a parent.

I cook a heap of chicken and put together a salad. I quickly eat some myself before putting the rest in containers to take around to Charlotte and Emmett. I imagine they're not going to feel up to cooking but that shouldn't mean they have to rely on disgusting takeaway.

Not wanting to disturb them, I leave it on their doorstep and send Charlotte a text.

I'm about to head home when a thought strikes me. Today wasn't the first time Bailey lied to me. At least, I'm pretty sure he's been lying about something else. Something to do with that locked room.

I walk up his driveway to the front door and knock, even though I know he isn't home. I peer through the window. Everything's dark inside.

With all the weird stuff going on, I can't help myself. I have to go inside.

I search the usual places for a spare key but the doormat and pot plants don't deliver.

The fence to his backyard is tall but so am I. And I don't spend hours in the gym for nothing. I can definitely climb it.

I land in the backyard on two feet, quietly impressed with myself. Stepping up onto the deck, the outdoor lounge stirs some feelings in me. Bailey's so sweet, we've had such a great time together. Why is he lying to me?

I hold my breath as I turn the handle on the back door. It opens. *Rookie.* Probably assumes the fence is unscalable and doesn't bother with the back lock. Bailey didn't turn off an alarm when we came home the other night but I hesitate anyway, waiting for some loud siren to go off and catch me breaking in.

*Seriously. What the hell am I doing?* There's no faster way to get your child taken off you than by being arrested for a crime. But I can't shake this feeling that there's something Bailey isn't telling me. What if it has something to do with Imogen?

A minute passes and there are no alarms or booby traps or any sign of police on their way so I use the torch on my phone to creep through the house.

Passing the kitchen, a half-finished mug of coffee and a piece of toast sit on the counter.

I get to the locked door and jiggle the handle, hoping it's been left unlocked as well. No such luck. I know I should leave but instead I go to his office at the front of the house. I pull out drawers and search cupboards. Then I spot a little wooden box on the shelf. It's painted black, with little gold carvings on it. I recognise the type of box immediately. It's a Hungarian puzzle box. My nana brought one home from Hungary for me when I was ten years old. I thought it was so special and I hid my best athletics ribbons in it.

I don't even know where mine is anymore and I've never seen another one since. I pick up the box and turn it over in my hands. It's exactly the same. I shiver. If he was going to hide something important, this would be the spot. No one knows how to get into these boxes unless they know about the combination of hidden panels. I push and twist and click the box in my hands until I've removed the secret panel revealing a key and lock. I open the box and there it is.

A single silver key on a wire loop.

I place the box back on the shelf and race back down the hall. Bailey could be home any minute and I'm not sure how I'd explain my presence. I left a bra? I forgot my toothbrush? He's not going to believe me and it certainly doesn't justify breaking and entering.

The key turns in the locked door and I pause.

I really don't know what to expect.

I'm pretty sure now that this isn't an office or a storage room, but what else would it be?

Maybe he's into some kinky sex stuff and he's keeping it a secret until he knows me better.

Perhaps he has a collection of rare and expensive comic books and figurines and he doesn't trust house guests.

But as I push open the door, I discover it's none of those things.

I flick the light switch this time because my torch isn't doing enough to illuminate the horror before me.

# PART II

# Chapter 26

## Amalia

'Is Jordy okay?' Imogen asks. She sits in the car seat in the back, eating the Happy Meal I bought her on the way out of Melbourne.

'He's fine, sweetheart.' I peer at her through the rear-view mirror. 'And I'm going to take good care of you.'

When I'd finally tracked down that truck a few weeks ago, I was horrified to discover the driver had children of his own. Knowing what he was capable of. Knowing he could kidnap a girl the same age as his own daughter. It was terrifying. But I had no proof and the police had already let me down. I decided to make it my responsibility to get Lila back. And what better way than with a trade.

His daughter for mine.

Imogen for Lila.

It's the perfect plan—I'll prove what a monster he is, get my daughter back, and Imogen will be safe without him in her life.

My hands slip on the steering wheel and my heart beats wildly in my chest as I imagine holding Lila again. I'm nervous. Of course I am—I've broken the law. Memories of the summer two years ago flash before me. It had been a hard few months as a new mother and I'd been desperate to fulfil my mum's dying wish to find a friend like she'd had. Her best friend Michelle was like a second mother to me. It seemed fitting to borrow Michelle's name the past few weeks.

*What will Paul think when he hears my plan?* The thought makes my stomach churn. I'm hoping he'll see sense and help me.

Paul and I moved into our dream home in Huntley when Lila was almost one. We'd only been together six months but he was the perfect, stable stepfather to Lil. And she needed it after a hectic start to her life. I wasn't interested in marrying anyone after what happened with my ex but when Paul proposed I knew it would be the best thing for Lila, and I finally felt safe and loved again. We got married soon after moving in together. He wanted to do the whole traditional wedding and party thing but I insisted on keeping it small and private.

We met when I was working at the pharmacy in Lakesfield. Somehow, we'd both lived in the quiet beach town for quite a while without crossing paths. He'd been travelling the previous summer, so he didn't know about what'd happened in the first few months of Lila's life. I've worked hard in the last couple of years to keep it that way.

Once we were married, Paul officially adopted Lila. The kindest thing my ex did for me was allowing that to happen. He had no relationship with Lila, so really, it was an easy way out from the financial burden of child support.

From the moment Paul and I met we always spoke about getting away from Lakesfield and living on a big property where Lila, and maybe someday, more kids, could run and ride around. A place where we could have plenty of pets and space to entertain. I think his time travelling sparked a love for nature and the outdoors. I was happy to go anywhere if it meant getting away from Lakesfield and the whispers. So it was a no-brainer to give up our small apartment near the ocean for a quaint little house on three acres of green fields.

Paul is the best thing to happen to Lila and me. I really hope he hears me out.

'Would you like to listen to The Wiggles?' I ask Imogen.

'No Wiggles.'

'But I've heard that's your favourite,' I say.

'No, I want Mummy.'

I hit play, ignoring her request. The Wiggles sing about hot potatoes and cold spaghetti. I glance at the rear-view again and can see her doing the actions. The hint of a smile on her face reminds me why I'm doing this. I'm saving two little girls today.

It's a long drive to Huntley and Imogen eventually nods off. Her lips pout out in the same way my Lila's do when she sleeps. My darling Lila. No one believes me that she's still alive, but I'm certain my baby is out there. I can feel it.

The police concluded that Lila had fallen in the creek, showing us her hat and a shoe that had shown up downstream. Seeing Lila's clothing like that had hurt, but I wasn't convinced. If someone is sick enough to take a child, they're sick enough to make it look like an accident. He could easily have thrown her things into the creek after snatching her.

Paul bought it, though. He said we should organise a memorial for Lila. I was outraged. The number of times I'd told him that it was the truck driver who visited our property that day who must have taken Lila was more than I could count. Paul didn't listen, he just went ahead and arranged the ceremony. On the morning of the memorial, I wrote him a note and left. I was going to find that truck and its driver, and find our daughter.

By the time I turn into our property, Imogen is asleep. She stirs when I unclip her from the car seat but doesn't cry. With Imogen in my arms, I walk through the front door of our family home.

'Paul!' I call. His car is out front so he must be inside somewhere. 'Paul, I'm back.'

'Amalia?' Paul says. I find him in our bedroom. His eyes widen when he sees who I'm carrying. 'Who's that?'

'Don't get mad,' I say.

'I'm serious, who is it?'

'Her name is Imogen.'

Paul rubs at his face. 'And?'

'And her father took Lila.'

He looks at me for a moment, not saying anything. Then he speaks slowly. 'What have you done?'

'I tracked down the truck driver and I took his daughter.'

Paul's jaw drops.

'Now we can trade,' I add.

'Amalia,' Paul says, his tone solemn. 'Are you okay? Have you been drinking? Taken something, maybe.'

I glare at him. 'I'm fine. Why aren't you happy? We're going to get Lila back.'

He closes his eyes and presses his fingers to his temples. When he opens them, tears spill over. 'Amalia, Lila is gone,' Paul says, his voice cracking. 'She's not coming back.'

I shake my head. 'No, you're wrong. She's alive, I know it. Just come back to Rosewood with me.'

'No,' he says. 'You're being ridiculous. I'm calling the police.'

'Paul, please don't do that. I know who has our girl. I'm so close!'

'You're crazy! I don't even know who you are anymore.' His voice is loud and it scares me. This isn't how I wanted it to go.

Imogen starts sobbing and I stroke her hair. 'It's okay, Immy. I'll take you home soon.'

'I'll get her some tissues,' Paul says, backing out of the room.

Why won't he help me? After everything I've done to make this happen. The hours I spent watching Charlotte's house and running around the park to *accidentally* bump into her. The fake smiles and friendly conversation I made to earn the woman's trust. The days I spent driving around her neighbourhood, taking note of her activities, putting her on edge, following her. And now Paul wants to call the police and blow our chances. How dare he! The cops let us down once. I'm not waiting around for them to mess it up again.

I know what I have to do. I place Imogen on the bed, slip into the walk-in wardrobe and find Paul's cricket bag. The rubbery handle of the cricket bat feels strange yet familiar in my hand.

I peek at the bedroom from behind the wardrobe door. Paul is back, wiping Imogen's face and whispering things I can't quite hear. She's nodding and trying to catch her breath between the little cries that escape her.

'Get away from her,' I yell, holding up the cricket bat like I'm ready to swing at a baseball.

'What the hell are you doing?' Paul says, jumping in front of Imogen.

'I'm stopping you from ruining this.'

'Amalia, don't be ridiculous! Put the bat down.'

I take a step closer. 'I'm serious. Move away from her.'

I watch as his mind ticks over, assessing his options. Then his eyes flick to something to the right. It's his pocket knife on the tall chest of drawers. He knows I've seen it too and makes a lunge for it. But he's too slow.

# Chapter 27

## Sloane

I squeeze my eyes shut, hoping my mind is playing tricks on me. But as I open them, I discover the horror is real.

One wall of the room is lined with computer monitors including three expensive-looking, wide screens. They flash with black-and-white images of dark rooms. No, not rooms—cells. And inside the cells are children.

I stumble back a step, distancing myself from what I'm looking at, hoping that'll help somehow, but it doesn't. Warm saliva fills my mouth and I swallow it back, pressing a hand hard against my breastbone. The screens keep flipping between the various cells so I can't tell how many children there are but it must be at least ten, maybe more. Some look as young as Frankie and others look like they could be in high school. Many of them are sleeping on the floor on piles of blankets. A few of them are sitting up. One girl is hugging her knees, rocking back and forth.

My body goes cold. I bolt to the bathroom and vomit. *What the hell is this?*

When my stomach stops rolling, I creep back to the room, terrified of what else I might find.

I avoid looking at the screens and approach the built-in closet. What will I find in there? A child? The taste of bile burns all the way down my throat.

Holding my breath, I yank open the doors. It looks like a normal closet—at least it would, if Bailey were a parent. The drawers and hangers are filled with kids' clothing in different sizes, for different seasons, all second-hand and well-worn. There's something unnerving about seeing full outfits hang there like this, the ghost of their owner lingering—perhaps on the screens behind me. Pairs of used shoes line the bottom of the closet and I'm reminded of a photo in one of my nana's albums. It was from the trip she took to Hungary. She'd also visited Auschwitz and photographed an exhibit that showed piles of shoes once worn by the prisoners. I choke back more burning liquid trapped in my throat.

At the top of the closet are containers labelled 'Books' and 'Toys'.

I pull one down and take off the lid.

A strangled scream escapes from my mouth.

I can't believe my eyes. It's filled with dolls.

Dolls just like the one Bailey gave me for Frankie.

*Who is this sicko?*

Jamming the lid back on, I place the container back where it was and quickly close the doors to the closet, cursing myself for touching evidence.

The screens draw me in again and I spot one I missed before, in the far corner of the room. I move closer; it doesn't have images of children on it like the others. It's a map of Melbourne and some of the surrounding regional areas. Sprinkled all over the map are red flashing icons. Most of them are stationary but one is moving, similar to how a car tracks along a road on Google maps.

I use the computer mouse to zoom in on Rosewood. There are two red icons in the area, one right next to where I am—Charlotte's house. *What the hell?* The other is ...

This time I don't make it to the bathroom before I'm sick again. Any hope I had of hiding my presence here has been destroyed by the pool of vomit now seeping into the carpet. I can't worry about that now. I have a phone call to make.

I open my phone up to recent calls and click on Tarkyn's name, my hands shaking.

'Hey. Any news?' he says when he answers.

'No.' My voice is tight. 'But I need you to check something for me.'

'Mmm?'

'You know the new doll Frankie has?'

'Yeah, she won't put it down. Currently cuddling it in bed.'

A few hours ago, I'd think this was adorable. Now, I can't think of anything more horrifying. 'I need you to go get it.'

He groans. 'Hold on.'

Footsteps float down the line and then silence. I stare at the red marker pinned to Tarkyn's street. The son of a bitch is tracking my child.

A moment later, there's a muffling sound. 'Got it.'

I gulp. 'Is there a battery pack or a zip or something on it?'

'Uh, the doll doesn't do anything fancy. It doesn't need batteries.' There's a pause. 'Hold on. There *is* something here.'

My heart races.

'Yeah. Looks like a really tiny battery pack but it's too small to actually have batteries. Not sure what it is.'

'Can you turn it on or off?'

'Yep.'

'Turn it off.'

There's a click and then, 'Done.'

The red circle on Tarkyn's house disappears from the screen and I cover my mouth. My entire body goes to jelly and I kneel down, hunched over on the floor, carefully avoiding where I've been sick.

'Sloane, what's going on?'

'I'm not sure. But I think I'm in danger.'

'What do you mean? You're scaring me.'

'I'm scared too.' And I have absolutely no one to turn to.

'Listen, Sloane. I know we aren't in a great place right now but you're the mother of my child, for god's sake. What can I do?'

Tears prick at my eyes. Tarkyn is offering to be there for me for the first time in a long time. 'Can you come and get me? I'll send you the address for where I am, it's next door to Charlotte's place. Leave Frankie with Janie, okay?'

'Okay. And hey, be careful.'

I take a deep breath. 'Call me when you get here. I'm calling the cops now.'

# Chapter 28

## Amalia

I place a hand on Paul's chest and release a sigh when there's a slight rise and fall. He's breathing but unconscious. A lump is already forming at his temple. I have no idea how long he'll be out of it so I need to move quickly.

'Come on, Immy,' I say, trying to grab her hand.

She's crying uncontrollably now. Shaking. When I finally get hold of her hand, she pulls it away.

'I'm so sorry I scared you, sweetheart. He was going to send you back to your daddy.'

'I want my daddy,' she wails.

'Come on. I know you're confused but we need to go now.'

'No!' She moves to the other side of the bed.

I'm trying to keep calm. I lunge for her and take hold of her arm. She screams.

'Hurting!' she says.

I keep my grip on her arm and lift her so that I can carry her out of the room. She throws her head back, screaming, and her legs kick at my thighs. When I get to Lila's bedroom, I put Imogen down. We installed a safety gate on the bedroom door a few months ago when Lila moved out of her cot and into a bed. After a few nights of finding her wandering around the house, helping herself to snacks and trying to get the television working, we thought it'd be safest to put the gate up. I close the gate now so that Imogen can't get out. This makes her scream and cry more. She grips the bars of the gate and tries to pull it open.

I bend down so that my head is level with hers. I reach out to caress her face but she steps back. 'I'm just going to pack a few things for us and then we can go.'

She says nothing. Better than 'no', I guess.

I go back to the bedroom. Paul is still lying there, motionless. I drag a suitcase out from under the bed. My stuff is still in the car, but I need Lila's things for when I get her back. I toss in some toys, books and snacks before returning to her bedroom. Imogen's sitting in the corner, cuddling one of the soft toys from the bed, a stuffed koala. I grab one of the other soft toys and put it in the suitcase, along with some clothes.

I'm putting all my weight on the overfilled suitcase, trying to zip it up, when I notice Imogen look up at the door suddenly. I turn around but there's nothing there. I pull the zip the remainder of the way and let out a breath.

'Done. Let's go.'

She stands up obediently, the koala still in her arms, and walks towards the door. I notice him a second too late.

'Run,' Paul shouts at her.

Imogen flees and he slams the gate behind her. *Shit.* I am perfectly capable of getting through the safety gate but my panicking fingers are slow to unlatch it and they're well beyond the front door by the time I get there. Paul isn't moving quickly, though—his concussion must be slowing him down. I can see Imogen just ahead of him on the driveway, running in the direction of the road.

'Keep running,' Paul calls to her as he slows to a stop. He bends over, hands on his upper thighs as though he's stopped to catch his breath. Then he falls to the ground.

My heart twists. He's my husband. And he's been the most amazing father to Lila for almost three years. Up ahead, Imogen is slowing down. Her little toddler legs are tiring on the long driveway. I make the decision to stop. I'll catch her, but first I need to make sure Paul is okay. As I bend down to put a hand on his chest and my ear to his mouth, his eyes shoot open.

His hand moves to his pocket. This time I'm not too late to notice.

I grab his fist as it moves towards me. He's clutching the pocket knife but he's so weak, so slow, that it requires no effort to shake it free from his hand.

'I stopped to help you,' I say, admonishing him.

'You're the one who needs help, Amalia.'

I shake my head, pocket the knife and leave him on the driveway.

When I catch up to Imogen, she's sitting down at the end of the driveway, crying.

I scoop her up and go back to the house, loading Imogen and the suitcase into the car. It's getting dark and the police will no doubt have worked out who I am and where I live, so I need to get out of here.

On the highway out of town, I pull over at a rest stop and call Charlotte.

# Chapter 29

## Charlotte

I don't sleep, although the police officers said I should.

*Get some rest. We'll call if anything changes.*

Are they insane? They think I'm going to be able to rest while my child is out there with a psycho?

Emmett sits on the couch beside me, absentmindedly flicking through channels on the television. I scroll through old photos of Imogen on my phone, using all my energy to hold it together. Every few minutes I jump up to check the driveway or the front yard.

'You know she's not here,' Emmett says after the third time.

'I know.' I sigh. 'I just thought, maybe it's all a misunderstanding and Michelle will drop her home.'

'*Amalia*,' Emmett corrects me. He takes my hand, giving it a squeeze. 'We'll get her back.' He offers a half smile. I don't think he's convincing himself, either.

It's about 9 p.m. and I'm watching an old video of Imogen's first crawl when my phone rings. The name 'Michelle' flashes up on the screen.

'Emmett,' I say. I glance over at him; he's mindlessly scrolling so I nudge him in the arm. 'Emmett. She's calling me.'

He jumps up. 'Well, what are you doing? Answer it.'

I answer and put it on speakerphone. 'Hello.'

'Hey, Charlotte. It's Michelle. Are you alone?'

'I know your name is Amalia,' I snap. 'Where's Imogen?'

Emmett winces at me and mouths the words *be nice*. I should probably be more polite—our child's life is in her hands—but I can't help it.

'Imogen's fine. Immy, come here and say hi to your mum.'

'Don't call her that!'

Then I hear my darling girl's soft voice. Her scared voice. 'Mummy.'

'Immy, honey. Are you okay?'

'Want to come home now.'

'I know. Me too.'

'It's okay, honey,' Emmett says and I shush him. What if Amalia only wants to speak to me?

'But Mummy. Moana says Daddy's bad.'

I glance at Emmett and he frowns.

'Don't listen to that. Daddy and I will see you soon.'

'Charlotte.' Amalia's voice returns, cold and venomous. 'I want to make a deal with you and your husband.'

'What do you want?'

'My daughter, Lila, was taken last month ... by your husband.'

A laugh bursts out of me and I clamp my hand over my mouth. I shouldn't laugh about her daughter's disappearance but it's ludicrous to suggest Emmett had anything to do with it.

'I'm sorry, what?'

'A man delivered some items to my property on the day Lila disappeared. He was driving a purple truck. I saw the same purple truck in your driveway a few weeks ago.'

'My husband is a paramedic. I've told you that before.'

'Maybe that's just what he tells you.'

'Amalia. My husband does not have a truck.'

Emmett shrugs and I whisper, 'she's crazy.'

'Charlotte, are you listening to me?' Amalia snaps.

'Yes. Emmett doesn't have a truck.'

'I saw him get out of it at your house. Be careful. Your children aren't safe.'

'This is insane. Bring Imogen home.'

'I will. I'm not a monster like your husband. Give me Lila and I'll return Imogen safely.'

I want to scream. The only way to get Imogen back is to give her what she wants. And we don't have what she wants.

I take a deep breath and try to remain calm. There's nothing I can do. Except maybe buy some time.

'Where are you?' I ask.

'I'm not going to tell you that.'

*Worth a try.* 'We'll meet you at Rosewood Parklands. When can you be there?'

'I'll meet you at seven tomorrow morning.'

I want to protest. A whole night away from my baby. But I feel more certain now that she won't hurt her, if only because she wants Lila back. Anyway, I don't plan on waiting until the morning.

'See you at seven. Can I speak to Imogen?'

There's a short pause.

'Mummy?'

'Immy, you're going to have a sleepover with Michelle, okay?'

'No. She hurt the nice man.'

*The nice man?* What is she talking about? 'Has she hurt you, sweet-heart?'

'No.'

'I will see you first thing in the morning, okay? I promise you it'll be okay.'

My heart aches as I picture her holding the phone, blinking back her tears. She's only two years old. She must be so scared.

'No, Mummy!' Imogen starts to cry and the call ends.

I burst into tears, my head in my hands. The sobs fall out of me, each one more painful than the last. I wait to feel Emmett's comforting arms around me but they don't come.

When I turn to him, his hand is over his mouth and he swears.

'What? What's going on?'

'I know what she's talking about.'

My eyes widen, demanding he continues.

'I borrowed Bailey's truck. The purple one. That's what she saw.'

'Oh,' I say, nodding as the memory floods back. The massive, garish vehicle was certainly distinctive. Imogen had even commented on how much she liked the colour.

'She must've followed me from the depot. That's the only time I came home with the truck.' He scratches at the stubble starting to form around his chin.

'Okay. Well, she said that a man delivered something to her house in that purple truck and took Lila.'

'That's Bailey's truck. He has lots of people do deliveries for him—not kidnappings.' He half laughs. 'I'll speak to him.'

I nod.

'So, what do we do?' he asks.

'You can call the cops if you want, but I'm not waiting until the morning to make a trade when we don't have Lila and she has some delusional idea that we do.'

'But we don't know where she is.'

'Imogen said she hurt the nice man. I'm not sure who the nice man is but I suspect it could be her husband. I reckon she's gone back to Huntley.'

'The local cops have already checked there.'

'Maybe they missed her. My gut says she's back there somewhere.'

'Charlotte, you can't go searching for her. She's dangerous.'

'I don't care. Emmett, this is our baby. I'm going to find her tonight.'

Emmett rubs his hand over his face. 'I'm not letting you go alone. You call the detective and I'll go see Bailey about the truck. Then we'll drive to Huntley together.'

I'm not thrilled with the plan. I want to leave right now. I want to get Amalia back on the phone and offer her every cent to our name, our house, a damn kidney so I can get Imogen back. But he's right. It's dangerous. We should go together.

# Chapter 30

## Sloane

I'm pacing the front room of Bailey's house in the dark, watching the street and praying that Tarkyn shows up first.

What would happen if Bailey found me here and realised I'd discovered his secret room? I'm not sure how he'd talk himself out of it. Or what he'd do to me now I know.

Our phone conversation from this afternoon runs on a loop in my mind. He *was* with kids, but not Imogen. It was the kids from the video footage. My stomach lurches again. Who knows who they belong to, or where they came from, or why they're there.

*Dammit.* How could I be so stupid? Bailey is attractive and charming and helps his neighbours. And on the side, he *what*? Kidnaps kids? Keeps them locked up? Then what does he do with them? I can't let my mind go there.

Headlights approach the house and light up the front room. I duck out of sight but I can still see the car. It's Tarkyn's. My body ripples with relief.

On cue, my phone rings.

'Hey,' I whisper. 'Come up to the house.'

Tarkyn gets out of his car, walks towards the house, then stops suddenly and turns around. Behind him, a tall figure approaches. My heart hammers in my chest. Is it Bailey?

The cops should already be on their way but I'm sure it wouldn't take long for Bailey to make us disappear and spin some story to the police. With the set-up he has, it's clear he's a professional criminal.

I still can't see the second person but based on their size, it has to be a man.

*Move, Tarkyn. Get away.*

Tarkyn and the man shake hands. The mystery person looks towards the house and the street lamp briefly lights up his face. It's Emmett. *Thank goodness.*

I open the door to Tarkyn and Emmett and they both look confused. Obviously, Tarkyn is expecting me but Emmett isn't.

'Sloane, what are you doing here?' Emmett asks.

'What are you doing here?' I counter.

'I need to ask Bailey something. Is he home?'

I shake my head. 'No. Is Imogen okay? Have you heard anything?'

'We've spoken to Amalia. She was saying some insane stuff about me kidnapping her daughter in a truck. I borrowed Bailey's truck a little while ago so I was coming over to ask him about it.'

'Holy shit,' I say slowly, registering what this means. The blood drains from my face. 'Come in.'

'Are you okay?' Tarkyn asks.

I shake my head. 'I don't think that story is as insane as you think, Emmett.' I take a deep breath, exhaling slowly as I try to compose myself. 'That poor woman. She was so close to finding her daughter. One house away.'

'What?' Emmett asks.

'Follow me,' I say, leading the men to the back room.

Before I open the door, I turn to them. 'What you're about to see is messed up. Just be aware.'

I open the door and flick on the light. No one says anything for a while. The stench of my vomit adds to the horror of the room. They look around, studying the monitors, taking in the tubs of toys and clothing, staring in disbelief at the children on the screens. I'm relieved that the girl who was crying and rocking earlier is now asleep. Hopefully this will be the last time she wakes up to this nightmare.

'What's this?' Emmett asks, pointing to the screen with the map on it.

'Tracking devices,' I say. 'There's one in your house. I suspect a toy that Bailey has given one of the kids. There was one in Frankie's doll. I don't know what the others are but they're spread far and wide.'

Emmett swears under his breath. 'That doll. Son of a bitch.'

'He was tracking Frankie?' Tarkyn asks. His face is grey and I wonder if I should let him know where the bathroom is.

I nod. 'I'm so sorry. I had no idea.'

'Who the hell is this guy?' he asks.

I really don't want to tell Tarkyn that I'd started dating this criminal. Luckily, Emmett speaks up first.

'Bailey. He's our neighbour. He mows the lawn and does washing for the old lady next door, has beers with us guys. He even looked after Immy the other day. I just, I can't …' Emmett runs a hand over his face. 'I just can't believe he would do anything to hurt anyone.'

'Sloane? How do you know him?'

*Dammit.*

'Does it really matter? All that matters is I found this stuff and now the cops can deal with it.'

'It *does* matter. My daughter—'

'Our daughter,' I correct him.

He glares at me. 'Frankie was being tracked by someone *you* know. Are you dating this guy?'

I shake my head. 'It's none of your business.'

'You're doing yourself no favours, Sloane. Do you even want to see your daughter?'

Emmett puts his hands up to signal us to stop. 'Look, guys. You two clearly have some stuff to sort out, but right now my daughter has been kidnapped and I've just found out my mate is involved in it somehow. Can you sort it out later?'

Tarkyn shakes his head. 'You'll be safe now Emmett's here. I better get back to Frankie. Keep me updated about Imogen, okay?'

I nod. He walks out and it takes all my willpower not to punch a hole in the wall.

My phone log says I called the police twenty minutes ago. Isn't that a long time to get to what must be a massive discovery for them? Bailey could come home at any minute.

'Charlotte called them too,' Emmett says when he sees me check my phone.

'Why?'

'Amalia told Charlotte that she won't give us Imogen until we return Lila.'

My jaw drops. *What the hell.* 'But you don't have Lila.'

'That's why we called the police.' He moves to the door. 'I need to get back to Charlotte.'

I nod and follow him out. Maybe I can wait at their house—I can't be here when Bailey gets back.

Red-and-blue lights flash as two police cars screech to the curb. We haven't made it off Bailey's property yet but it's okay. The police are here now. I'm safe.

A woman introduces herself as Detective Kitchen and from the way she greets Emmett, it's clear they already know each other. Three other officers in uniform introduce themselves as well. I'm about to take them inside when Charlotte bolts across the nature strip. Her face is red and blotchy.

'You're at the wrong house,' she says. Her tone is manic, high-pitched. The kind of voice that haunts you. Then she sees me. 'Sloane. What are you doing here?'

Emmett puts an arm around her. 'Charlotte, honey, you should wait inside.'

Charlotte pushes Emmett away. 'No. Where's Imogen?'

Emmett doesn't answer.

'Emmett, why are you just standing there? What the hell is going on?'

'The police haven't spoken to me about Imogen yet. Something else has happened.'

'What could be more important than finding our baby?' Charlotte's fists clench at her sides.

Emmett calmly takes her hands in his and she slowly releases the fists. 'Just trust me. Come back inside,' he says.

'No, we're going to Huntley, remember?'

'Things have changed,' he says, leading her back inside their house.

'Sloane, I believe you made the discovery?' Detective Kitchen asks and I don't hear the rest of Charlotte and Emmett's conversation.

'Yes.' My voice is shaky. In fact, my entire body is trembling and I put my hand on the brick letterbox to steady myself.

'What were you doing here?'

I don't want to lie to the police but I know I should've called them the moment I suspected something. So I run with the same story I'd planned to tell Bailey.

'I left my bra here.' My face flushes. Thank goodness Tarkyn isn't here. 'I just used the spare key to go in and get it.'

'And the room. You mentioned on the phone it was locked?'

Why does this even matter? Why am I being interrogated? They should be giving me a bloody medal for finding that room.

'Yeah. I unlocked it when I couldn't find my bra. Thought maybe Bailey put it in there.'

Detective Kitchen nods and narrows her eyes. She doesn't believe me.

I don't care. She'll be patting me on the back in a minute.

I lead the police inside and they ask me to wait in the living room. I want to go home but they say they might have more questions.

When Detective Kitchen emerges, her face is ashen. 'Do you have any idea where Bailey is now?'

I shake my head. 'No. He told me earlier that he was at work.'

'What does he do for work?'

'I don't really know, it's a family business. I think he usually works from home.'

She lifts an eyebrow and scribbles in her notebook. Surely she doesn't think I'm okay with this. I'm not the Bonnie to his Clyde in this situation.

The detective asks a few more questions about Bailey's habits, connections. I don't know the answers—all I can think is what an absolute idiot I am for dating this guy. Finally, she closes her notebook.

'Thanks. Can you see one of the officers on your way out so we can take down your details? We'll need to get a formal statement at some stage. Then you can go.'

I do as I'm told but I don't really know where to go next. I'm scared to be alone. Lately, when I'm feeling upset or overwhelmed, I call Bailey. But that would be stupid. Dangerous.

I dial his number.

# Chapter 31

## Amalia

I'm still parked at the rest stop, trying to figure out my next move, when two police cars speed past in the direction of my house. It won't be long before they find Paul and he explains everything.

I pull out onto the highway and within a minute, Imogen falls asleep. What a relief. One less thing to worry about. And there is *so much* to worry about right now. I wouldn't be able to focus if she was crying in the back seat.

I'm certain that Charlotte would've called the police after I spoke to her. To be honest, I don't even care. Perhaps the police will actually do something now. Maybe they'll finally take me seriously. I don't intend to hurt Imogen—I'd never hurt a child. But I had to do something to get Lila back. I'm sure I can expect more than a slap on the wrist for this. I've no doubt they'll lock me up. But it's worth it if Lila is okay. She'll be with Paul, and eventually I'll get out and be with them. If he takes me back.

An exit sign looms and I indicate into the off ramp. It'll take me the long way back to Melbourne and Rosewood but the police will be looking for me on the main road and I'm so close to getting Lila. I need to get back to Rosewood before they find me. I'm tempted to steal a car and finish the drive in something less recognisable but I don't want to add grand theft auto to my rap sheet. That'll keep me away from Lil even longer.

I'm about an hour out of Melbourne when my phone rings. It's Charlotte. I don't want to wake Imogen by taking the call through the car speakers so I pull over and get out to answer. It's a quiet country road. There are no street lamps and with my headlights off, I'm basically invisible. I keep the door open a crack in case Imogen stirs, and lean against the bonnet.

'Yes?' I answer.

'Hey. Where are you?'

'Charlotte, I told you before. I'm not going to tell you where I am. I'll see you at seven like we planned.'

'Wait, though. Things have changed.'

Now we're getting somewhere. 'What?' I ask.

'I think I know who has Lila.'

My heart races. 'You finally realised your husband is a creep?'

Charlotte exhales loudly into the phone. 'No. It's someone else. We've found something.'

Charlotte explains what was found in her neighbour's house: screens, CCTV footage, kids' clothes. My chest tightens and I struggle to take in air. What the hell has my poor baby been caught up in? I pace the length of the car, desperately trying to breathe steadily.

'Amalia, are you there?'

'Yes,' I croak.

'The police are handling it. They'll find her.'

'Did you see her? Is she okay?'

'I didn't go in there. Plus, I don't know what your daughter looks like.'

I blink back tears, picturing Lila's angelic face. Her blond hair bouncing as she runs around the yard. A huge smile lighting up the room and her cheeky little voice telling stories about anything and everything.

A guttural moan escapes me, releasing all the pain I've been holding back over the last few weeks. And in that moment, I feel more than sadness. I feel guilty. This agony is indescribable and I've caused the same pain for Charlotte. 'I'm so sorry,' I choke out between sobs. 'You know I'd never have hurt Imogen, don't you?'

'You kidnapped her,' she snaps. 'No, I don't know that and I don't know you at all. Just bring her home now. The police can help you get Lila back. This has nothing to do with my family.'

I don't see any point in waiting anymore. Emmett didn't do it. Wishful thinking, but I'd hoped we could hand over the girls and sweep it under the carpet. Tell the police it was a misunderstanding. Pretty far-fetched, maybe, but no harm done, right?

Now, there's no escaping the fact that I need the police and the police want me. If I'm going to get Lila back, I need to turn myself in.

'You can tell the police that I'll be there in an hour.'

Charlotte sobs, and the sound pierces my heart.

# Chapter 32

## Charlotte

I pace back and forth in front of our house, my hands trembling every time I check my phone for a message or call from Amalia. *What if she changes her mind? What if she doesn't bring Immy home?* I shake the thought out of my head. If Amalia feels anything like I do right now, she'll be doing whatever she can to get her child back. I flick the blinds shut. Now is not the time to worry about Lila and those poor children—the police can take care of that. I need to focus on Imogen, make sure she's okay. Make sure she knows she's safe and that I'll move heaven and earth to keep it that way.

The sound of a car steals my attention from the hundredth glance at my phone. It's another police car pulling up in front of Bailey's place. There are so many officers here now. I suppose at any stage, one of two criminals—or maybe both—will round that corner.

'Dammit,' I say under my breath, but Emmett hears me.

He walks over and puts an arm around my shoulders.

'I thought she'd be here by now. Maybe she isn't coming. What if she changes her mind?' The words tumble out and my chest constricts, making it hard to take a breath.

Emmett says nothing, just holds me a little tighter. I need him to tell me it's going to be okay, that I'm worrying about nothing, of course she's coming. But his silence is deafening and with every passing minute, Imogen feels further and further out of reach.

Most of the police officers have been moving in and out of Bailey's house. I try to switch my focus to them, hoping it'll distract me. Officers in uniforms and plain clothes enter. Some of them come back out carrying evidence bags and boxes. One man comes out looking green. He leans against the front fence before emptying the contents of his stomach onto the driveway. I don't need this kind of distraction. I take another look at my phone. It's almost midnight.

'Mrs Jenkins?' Detective Kitchen is stalking across the lawn towards me. 'I've been updated on the latest situation.'

'Has something else happened?' I ask.

'No. Nothing more since your phone call with Amalia. You should not be sharing information about the crime scene at your neighbour's place.'

My eyes narrow. 'What? Why?'

'The information is to be shared if and when the police choose to do so. And certainly not with another known criminal. What if they're in on it together?'

I shake my head. 'They're not. This is totally separate. Surely you know that.'

'We can't rule it out yet, and you could have compromised the entire operation. It's important that you let the police handle this now. When Amalia arrives, you are not to approach her.'

My cheeks burn. I feel like a child being chastised at school. I'm a victim here. My child has been kidnapped. And she has the nerve to lecture me on police protocol? Nope. No way. If I see Imogen, nothing and no one will stop me going to her.

\*\*\*

Just after midnight, a familiar white SUV turns into our street. It comes to a stop in the middle of the court and the police approach, guns drawn.

'Keep your guns lowered until we have the child,' an officer says.

I run towards the road but Emmett's arms close around me before I reach the curb. I try to fight him off; I need to get to Immy.

'Let the police handle this. You heard the detective.'

Tears stream down my cheeks. I need to hold my baby, *now*. 'Imogen!' I scream.

'Stay back, please, Mrs Jenkins,' one of the officers calls to me.

Emmett squeezes me tightly and I stop fighting him.

Through the front windscreen, I can just make out Amalia raising her arms as an officer opens the door. She steps out and an officer moves in quickly to handcuff her. As he pulls her arms behind her back, our eyes lock.

This is Michelle. The kind woman who told me I was doing a great job. Who helped me with the pram, with the shopping.

She's been so friendly.

My skin crawls as I realise how easy it was for her to infiltrate my world.

Two police officers take Amalia into Bailey's house. I'd heard the detective saying earlier that they'd allow her to identify if Lila was in any of the footage. I suppose that's fair, even though I want her sent straight to a cell of her own, like she deserves.

A third officer opens the back door of the car and waves over one of the paramedics standing by.

My breath hitches. Immy must be hurt. I claw my way out of Emmett's grasp and run to the side of the car. The police officer puts her hand up, signalling me to stop.

'What is it? What's wrong with her?' I plead.

'Doesn't appear to be harmed at all,' the paramedic says.

My legs almost give way from the relief.

The policewoman picks up a sleepy Imogen. She blinks a few times and smiles. They hand her over to me and she rests her head on my shoulder.

'Mummy.'

'Yes, sweetheart, I'm here. Are you okay?' I ask, smothering her in kisses.

Emmett wraps his arms around both of us.

'I'm okay. Why are you sad?'

'I'm not sad. These are happy tears. We're so happy you're home.' I brush her hair out of her eyes. She looks exhausted. 'Are you hungry?'

'No. Moana gave me Donald's.'

'McDonald's, hey?' Emmett says. 'You lucky girl.' A tear runs down his cheek.

Imogen giggles. Well, at least she doesn't seem too traumatised. Can't say the same for myself.

We take her inside and I lay her on the couch next to me. There is no way I'm letting her out of my sight. She's asleep on my lap in minutes.

Emmett sits next to us.

It's hard to comprehend the events of the night, to piece it all together. Emmett had described the room at Bailey's house, those children on the screens, but it doesn't seem real. I look down at Imogen's face, so peaceful. 'You know we're the lucky ones, yeah?'

He sighs. 'I know. I've seen some pretty horrific things at work but what I saw in Bailey's house tops it all.'

The red-and-blue lights still flash outside, lighting up our kitchen and living room.

'I'll call Katya and our families. Then I'm going to bed,' Emmett says.

I nod and scoop up Imogen to take her into our room. A loud scream comes from outside and through the window I spot Amalia staggering out of Bailey's house, flanked by two officers. She's crying hysterically, her whole body shaking. It's painful to watch. Her hands are still cuffed behind her and she can't wipe her face or hold anything to steady herself. She collapses to her knees in Bailey's front yard.

Lila must be on one of those screens.

# Chapter 33

## Sloane

The first call doesn't connect. Then an officer knocks on my window. He explains that I can't leave yet for my safety. Do they know something about Bailey? But then a white SUV passes me and I see Imogen reunited with Charlotte and Emmett in my rear-view mirror. I smile and the officer waves me through.

I call Bailey again.

The phone rings as I drive up his street and around the corner in the L-shaped court. I don't know where I'm headed. I don't even know what I'm going to say to him.

Turns out I don't have long to think about it. He doesn't answer but as I turn out of the street, my car almost collides with his. I slam on my brakes and stare at him through my windscreen. He looks back at me, beaming.

He has no idea that when he rounds the corner at the bottom of his street, he'll see a wall of red and blue flashing lights. There'll be guns drawn, there'll be demands that he doesn't move. He'll be cuffed and taken away, locked up for a very long time.

I force a smile that makes my stomach churn because I need him to stay here a moment longer. I need to know why.

Pressing the button to put my window down, I motion to him to do the same. He takes my hint as I edge my car alongside his.

'What are you doing here so late?' he asks.

I don't allow myself to panic. I ignore the way his eyes shine in the moonlight and how his curls fall messily around his perfect face.

'I was with Charlotte. They just found Imogen.'

Bailey slumps back in the seat of his car, visibly relaxing. He runs a hand through his hair. 'Thank God,' he whispers.

How can a man who abducts children, keeps them as prisoners and does who-knows-what with them be so visibly relieved about this? It makes no sense to me.

Tears well in my eyes and I look away.

His engine shuts off and I turn back to see him climbing out of his car. We are completely blocking the road in and out of his street. My heart races. What the hell is he doing?

'It's okay, Sloane. They found her.' He opens my car door and I realise he's trying to comfort me. He thinks my tears are for Imogen. 'Come here,' he says, reaching for me.

I pull away. 'Don't touch me.'

His eyes narrow and he steps back. 'What's wrong?'

I squeeze the steering wheel in front of me, forcing out my fear and finding strength to do this.

'How could you do it?'

'Do what?'

My heart is thumping in my chest. I wonder if he can hear it. 'I went into your house. Got in through the back.'

His hands clench at his sides and he looks down the street in the direction of his house.

'I also found the puzzle box and the key to the back room.'

He starts shaking his head. 'It's not what you think, Sloane.'

I blink back the tears that are coming quickly now. 'I don't know what to think.' My body is trembling. I keep my grip on the steering wheel, using it to anchor me.

'I'm involved in something bad. Really bad. And I can't get out of it.'

'What do you mean?'

He says nothing for a moment, fidgeting with a button on his shirt.

'I took over Dad's freight company when he died last year. Remember, I told you that I wanted to change things?' He steps closer to the car.

'Stay there.'

He continues. 'Dad borrowed money from some dangerous people. They made a deal with him. He started using the trucks for other purposes and managing their activities, and in return, my dad's debt was cleared. Then he got greedy and kept going. He was paid very well.' Bailey rubs his face and I notice the stubble is even longer now. 'I've tried to get out of it but they make threats.'

'But, you're helping them. You gave me a doll to track Frankie. And you were tracking Imogen.'

He nods. 'Because I care about Imogen and I care about you. I never know who they're going to take but I thought if I was a part of their lives and keeping an eye on them, they'd be safe.'

'What about the teething ring? Charlotte reckons it's what caused Jordy's reaction. You could've killed him.'

'I didn't know about that at the time,' he says, rubbing the back of his neck. 'They were with me when I took a call from Emmett about dinner at his house, and he mentioned Jordy's allergy. They deliver goods to my house and probably took a punt with the teething rings. When I saw them, I thought, perfect, they might help the little guy. I was set up. They wouldn't have liked me getting close to people like that.' Bailey is breathing quickly now. Panicking.

'That doesn't even make sense! Stop lying.'

'Sloane, I'm not a bad guy.'

I shake my head. 'There's nothing you can say that makes this okay.'

Bailey's expression changes at that. His blue eyes are no longer friendly, they're cold. His lips are no longer twisted with remorse, they curl up in a way that makes my skin prick. He takes another step closer. His eyes are level with mine, only a metre away from me in the front seat of my Jeep.

'Stop,' I say, my voice low and hard.

'I didn't want it to come to this, Sloane.' Another step closer.

I glance at my phone on the passenger seat. Could I reach it before he gets to me?

'I'm sorry it has to be this way.' His words slice through me.

I lunge for my phone but I've barely moved before he slams me back against the seat, his hands around my neck. I grab at his wrists, trying to pull him off. He takes one hand away and uses it to restrain my hands.

'It's too late,' I splutter. 'You're too late.'

He presses harder against my neck. 'I was going to protect Frankie and you've betrayed me?'

He seems genuinely shocked by this. Did he think I was that much of a pushover? Did he think I'd just turn a blind eye?

I kick my right leg out to the side, trying to connect with his knees, but I'm in such an awkward position, I can't reach. All that jiu-jitsu training can't help me now.

'Stop fighting me, Sloane. It's over for you.'

I struggle to take a breath. Spots begin to cloud my vision. I kick out again, pain coursing through my hips where the seatbelt digs in.

This time my foot makes contact and his grip on my hands loosens. 'No, it's over for you,' I grit out. I reach for the horn in front of me and press down hard until Bailey rips my hand away. The blast fills the air around us and immediately, lights flick on in nearby houses.

But it's not the people in the houses whose attention I'm trying to get.

Bailey lets me go and clambers back into his car. He starts it up and slams the car into reverse. Just as his car starts backwards up the street, a police car flies around the corner from the direction of his house.

I press on the horn again, desperate for the police to understand. *This is your man. Hurry up.*

Bailey reaches the top of the street and speeds away.

# Chapter 34

## Amalia

As soon as I identified Lila on the screens in that man's house, the police took me back to the station and put me in a small room. I'm no longer in handcuffs, thank goodness. They'd been digging into my wrists and it was so hard to keep upright and balanced, especially after seeing footage of Lila alone in a cold, empty cell.

The room I'm in has a couch and the detective brought me some water and a pack of biscuits. Not bad, considering I kidnapped a child today.

There has been no updates on Lila, though, and it's killing me. I can't stop thinking about what I saw on the computer monitor in that room. *What has my baby been through?*

The room has a window that looks out at the reception area of the police station. It's hard to tell what's going on because there are so many people moving around.

Detective Kitchen steps into the room, holding up her mobile. 'I've got your husband on the phone,' she says.

I stand up. I'm dying to speak to Paul, but does he want to talk to me after what I did to him? I stare at the detective and bite my lip.

She nods. 'He wants to speak to you.'

I rush over and grab the phone.

'Paul?'

'Hey.'

'Paul, I'm so sorry.'

'No,' he says, and I can tell that he's crying. '*I'm* sorry. The police filled me in about Lila. I should've believed you. You were so sure she'd been taken and I told you to drop it.'

I say nothing. It broke my heart not having Paul's support.

'I'm on my way to Rosewood now. An officer is driving me. I'll be with you soon, okay?'

A sob escapes my throat. Slowly, the weight of the last few weeks is lifting off my shoulders. I don't have Lila back yet but Paul will be here.

'Paul, I'm sorry—'

'Stop. Listen, I told the police about how you came home briefly this afternoon and you were mad with me for not believing you. You sped off and I tripped chasing you down the driveway.'

I blink back tears. He lied for me.

'I love you, Paul,' I whisper.

'I love you, too. I'll be there soon.'

I hand the phone back to the detective. She slides it into her pocket and gives me a small, kind smile. 'Our officers have Bailey in custody. They're bringing him in now. We should know where your little girl is very soon.'

'Thank you.' The tears spill over. 'And what will happen to me?'

'Well, you abducted a child. There'll be criminal charges and it'll be up to the courts to decide.'

She walks out and I'm left to ponder that. *Criminal charges*. It's what I deserve and what I expected, after all. But it no doubt means more time away from Lila and Paul, when Lila needs me more than ever. My heart aches and I drop my head into my hands and sob.

\*\*\*

I sit on the couch in the small room, my mind cycling between worry and relief, for what feels like hours. Finally, there's a knock at the door and Detective Kitchen enters with Paul. He looks terrible—his eyes are bloodshot and his face is haggard. I rush over to him and throw my arms around his neck. He winces.

'I'm sorry,' I say. 'I'm so sorry.'

He shakes his head.

'That fall really did a number on you,' Detective Kitchen says, lifting an eyebrow. 'Do you need a doctor?'

I say 'yes' at the same time he says 'no'.

'Paul, you should get checked out,' I say.

'No need, I'm fine.' His eyes plead with me to drop it.

*Of course*. If he gets checked, they'll discover he was actually hit with a hard, blunt object. And that doesn't match his story.

I nod and turn to the detective. 'Any news on Lila?'

'The team is moving in shortly. We'll have news any minute now.'

I take a deep breath. I feel sick thinking about what Lila must be going through. She's been in that place for three weeks now. Is she being fed? Is she warm enough? Has she been scared this whole time? Paul pulls me in for a hug and the tears come again.

'I'll leave you two alone,' Detective Kitchen says. 'I'll be back when I know more.'

Paul walks me over to the couch and we sit down, our bodies close.

'Are you in trouble?' he asks.

I struggle to return his gaze. 'Yes.'

'We'll work it out.'

He draws me close and we sit like that on the couch for hours. We don't speak, we barely move. I just stare straight ahead out the window at the reception area. As the night wears on, the foot traffic slows. Then it picks up again with some urgency, but still, no updates. I'm about to bang on the window when Detective Kitchen opens the door.

'I have someone here to see you.'

I jump up, my wobbly legs barely keeping me upright.

A female police officer walks in with Lila in her arms. She puts her on the ground but Lila stays close to her. My heart sinks. Why isn't she coming over to us?

'Lila has had a traumatic few weeks,' the detective says. 'Give her some time.'

I walk over and bend down in front of her. 'Lil, it's Mummy.'

For the first time, she looks at me. Her hair is matted and she's wearing dirty pyjamas that have a hole in one of the knees. Recognition flashes in her eyes.

She takes a tiny step closer to me.

'Mummy.' Her voice is barely a whisper.

Tears run down my cheeks as I put my hand out. Lila places her little hand in mine. It's cold and I give it a gentle squeeze.

'Mummy. I'm sorry.'

I pull her in and wrap my arms around her. Then I lift her up to my waist so that she's eye level with me, drinking in the face I've missed so much. Paul shuffles beside us and gives Lila's arm a gentle rub.

'Lila, you have nothing to be sorry for,' I tell her.

'The man said I could help with Daddy's work stuff.'

My heart cracks. She always wants to help Paul in the shed. 'You did nothing wrong, darling. That was a bad man. You're safe now.'

# Chapter 35

## Sloane

### Six weeks later

'Frankie, honey, it's time to go.'

'Cooomiiing,' she calls.

We're running late for our mothers' group catch-up. A few months ago, I'd have been spiralling at the thought of not being punctual. Now, it takes quite a lot more to rattle me. I suppose when you discover a child-trafficking ring in your boyfriend's spare room, you no longer sweat the small stuff.

It's also a great way to become somewhat of a local hero and get your ex back on side. It seems most people forget that I was dating Bailey, that complete and utter sicko, or they're pretending it didn't happen so as not to embarrass me. I wouldn't say I'm embarrassed, though. Anyone could fall for his looks and charm. Are all women meant to search their dates' houses to rule out signs of organised crime before sleeping with them now?

The main thing is, Tarkyn has cooled his jets when it comes to the custody battle. We're sticking to fifty-fifty custody and communicating regularly, without snarky comments or sneaky trips to the zoo to make one another jealous. *Still not quite over that one.*

Frankie runs down the hallway carrying her new doll. We had to replace the one Bailey gave her, partly because it became evidence and partly because ... gross! My child is not playing with an item intended to lure innocent children away from their parents when they're not watching. She'd been devastated to lose her precious new doll, so a trip to the toy store had been inevitable. And even though I knew it was silly, I frisked the new doll for secret battery packs and tracking devices. Perhaps that habit will never leave me.

'What took you so long?' I ask Frankie as she slips her hand in mine.

'Baby needed wee-wee.'

Of course it did. Another area of my life where I've had to relinquish control. Frankie is obsessed with the toilet and underwear, but she isn't toilet trained yet so I'm forever cleaning up puddles. Tarkyn and Janie want to put her through an intensive three-day, stay-home toilet-training program but I couldn't care less. She'll figure it out. I don't remember anyone coming to school in a nappy, so it must happen somehow.

We hop in the car and drive to the playground to meet the other mums. Today is only our second catch-up since Imogen was kidnapped—it took a while for Charlotte to feel comfortable leaving the house again, understandably. I'd been nervous to see everyone when we caught up two weeks ago. I was the fool who fell for the criminal, so I figured they'd all be judging me. But, hey, Charlotte had befriended both Bailey and Amalia, so they couldn't judge me without judging her, and you can't judge the mum whose child was kidnapped.

As it turned out, when we'd gotten together, things were mostly normal. We drank coffee and listened to the toddlers and babies giggle, cry, complain and gobble down snacks as though they hadn't eaten in weeks. Imogen had stayed home with Emmett that time. Charlotte wasn't ready to take her out yet, and she only stayed for five minutes with Jordy. A quick hello. Not long enough to really gauge how she was going.

By the time we arrive at the park, Katya has already set up a spot on the grass and Levi and Oscar are playing. Iris pulls up a few spaces away and calls to me from behind her car as she unloads Billy and the twins. We walk over together and Billy and Frankie make a beeline for the play equipment.

'Is Charlotte coming today?' I ask, knowing that Katya will have spoken to her.

'Yep. And she's bringing Imogen. Emmett's at work.'

I smile. 'Lovely. I haven't seen her since …' I trail off. I don't like saying it aloud. 'Well, you know.'

Charlotte arrives a few minutes later, pushing a double pram that I haven't seen before. Usually Imogen rides her trike or sits on the toddler skateboard behind the pram, but today she's strapped in next to her brother.

We exchange hellos before Iris leaves to do the coffee run.

Charlotte places Jordy on the blanket next to Oscar and the twins. Jordy wriggles around until he's in a crawling position. He stays that way for a few seconds before his arms give way and he flops to the ground, giggling. Imogen stays cuddled up in Charlotte's arms.

'Do you want me to take you over to see Frankie?' I ask her.

Charlotte shakes her head. 'No, Imogen's not up to playing today.'

'Sure,' I say, a little confused. 'I see you got a new pram. What made you get the double?'

Charlotte looks over at the big pram parked beside her. 'I just like having the kids confined when we're out and about. Immy was getting too far away on her trike, you know?'

I nod slowly and a heaviness settles in my chest.

'Are you okay?' I ask.

Charlotte flashes a tight smile. 'Getting there.'

I'm guessing Imogen hasn't been out of Charlotte or Emmett's sight, or even arm's reach, since the incident. And for a little kid, that must be scary. I hated seeing my dad upset. I can't imagine what Immy has seen.

'Im! Im!' Frankie shouts as she bounds over from the playground.

Imogen turns her head and beams when she sees Frankie. She tries to stand up but Charlotte pulls her back down. Imogen frowns.

'Mummy, I want to play.'

'Not now, sweetheart.'

Imogen buries her head in Charlotte's lap and cries. I thought I could handle any kind of heartache after seeing those children on the computer screens but this is painful to watch.

Then I get an idea.

'I'll be right back,' I say, jumping up.

I dash over to my car, grab what I need from the boot and jog back to the group.

'Here, you can have this,' I tell Charlotte, handing her a toddler hiking backpack.

She takes it, looking confused.

'I know you have a baby carrier for Jordy but this is for bigger kids. You put it on your back. I use it when I take Frankie hiking. This way you can put Immy on your back. You can put her in now and we can go on the swings or the spinner.'

She tilts her head, contemplating what I've said. 'I don't know, Sloane.'

*Ugh, come on. Let me help you.*

'That's a great idea,' Katya says.

*Yes! Back-up.* I shoot her a grateful look.

'Let's just try it on and then you can decide about the playground,' I say.

Charlotte nods and I help her get Imogen onto her back. Then I strap her carrier to me and take Jordy. Both kids confined. This is good.

Imogen giggles from her mum's back. 'Mummy, I'm the queen.'

Charlotte's shoulders relax and she smiles. 'Well, best we go find you a castle, then.' And she walks over to the playground.

I go to follow with Jordy but Katya grabs my hand and pulls me back.

'Let them go, I think,' she says, her eyes shining with tears.

Iris returns with the drinks but Charlotte's coffee goes cold as she spends the next half hour running around the playground with Imogen on her back.

'I don't think they've smiled this much in a long time,' Katya says. 'Thank you, Sloane.'

'Us mums have to stick together.' I smile and silently promise to make more of an effort with these women, my *friends*. Not just for Frankie anymore. For me.

# Chapter 36

## Charlotte

### Six months later

I barely recognise the woman staring back at me in the mirror. The past six months have changed me. The soft curves of my postpartum body have been replaced with sharp hips that protrude from my slim frame. My full cheeks are now angular and harsh and the skin under my eyes is permanently stained deep purple.

After Imogen came home, I was relieved, of course. Then the news stories started, highlighting the way I'd been manipulated—how I'd put too much trust in strangers. I thought Michelle—no, *Amalia*—was my friend but she'd stalked me in her car just to scare me so she could get close to me. I thought I could trust Bailey, but he'd given Jordy peanut, almost killing him. I thought I could rest knowing my daughter was safe at childcare, but they handed Immy over to a criminal without a second thought. I was a fool.

From then on, I decided I'd always be watching. Every day, my kids are with me. Every night, I sleep on the floor between their bedrooms on a roll-out foam mattress. I've lost weight and I barely sleep, but at least I know they're safe. Emmett has given up trying to convince me that everything's okay and that I can sleep in my own bed.

If something happened to them, I could never forgive myself. I still haven't forgiven myself for what *did* happen.

Emmett enters the bathroom, his reflection appearing next to mine. He looks the same, as though the last six months were like the six before that and the year before that.

He straightens his tie. 'Are you sure you want to do this, Charlie?' he asks, placing a gentle hand on my back.

I want to take the opening as a chance to bail on today, to stay with the kids and hide from it all, but my therapist thinks it could help. My parents are going to look after the kids and Katya is coming around as well. That's three fully capable adults who will not take an eye off my children, but I'm still scared. It'll be the first time they've been away from Emmett or myself since that day.

'I need to,' I reply, barely a whisper.

'Okay. Then we better get going.'

I nod and put on my coat.

Outside the courthouse, news reporters are swarming. I've avoided speaking to the media so far and I don't intend to change that today.

The morning is icy cold and I shiver under my thick woollen coat as we hesitate on the pavement. Emmett slings a tight arm around me. We put our heads down, pushing through the cameras and microphones thrust at us until we're inside the courthouse.

Sloane is already there and she repeats the same question Emmett asked at home.

'Are you sure you want to do this?'

I smile at her. Sloane's different these days. No longer do I feel judged or intimidated by her. Now, she's relaxed. She's fun and care-free. We've had two mothers' group dinners out where we splurged on delicious food and wine and she didn't blink an eye. And to top it off, she brings Imogen a babycino every second Friday when she has Frankie. Yep, those sugar bombs are now a staple in Frankie's diet too.

'I want to be here,' I say firmly. 'You?'

Sloane's smile is wicked. 'Absolutely. I want to see this creep pay.'

Bailey pleaded guilty to being an accessory to kidnapping, human trafficking and the attempted murder of Sloane. He hadn't been the one to take Imogen but it was his actions that set the ball rolling and gave Amalia a motive to take Immy. Ultimately, he was to blame. Not to mention the personal betrayal, because we thought he was our friend. The charges for deliberately giving Jordy peanut didn't stick. The evidence was apparently insubstantial.

We shuffle into the hard wooden seats of the courtroom, myself between Emmett and Sloane. I can feel the stares of the other people in the room. *Yes, we're the fools who trusted this man with our kids*, I think. *Yes, she's the fool who dated him*. But fool is a harsh word; Bailey was an expert manipulator. Charming. The perfect neighbour. Gosh, it almost killed Mags when she found out.

When Bailey is escorted into the courtroom, Sloane inhales sharply and I grab Emmett's hand. Bailey's blond curls are gone, his hair is shaved short and he's grown a beard, ageing him about twenty years. His face is stony.

Most of the hearing is a blur. The prosecution details Bailey's crimes and I try not to absorb it. I close my eyes and suck in deep breaths, imagining the voice of my therapist talking me through a panic attack. I've heard enough in the news and from the articles Iris was sending me. I had to tell her to stop, that I didn't want to know anything else. The details were too disturbing.

Then the defence starts. Surely, there's nothing to defend?

But then there are words thrown around that take my breath away.

*Cooperation.*

*Remorse.*

*Reduced sentence.*

'Son of a bitch,' Sloane whispers.

We all knew Bailey was just a pawn in a larger organised crime ring but it doesn't seem right that he can wriggle out of his punishment by 'cooperating'.

When the hearing is over, I'm numb. Bailey will be in prison for a long time. My babies will be adults before he's released, which brings me a small amount of comfort. But he wasn't given the maximum sentence.

Bailey doesn't even have the guts to look at us as the police march him out of the dock. Emmett tenses next to me, watching him go. He thought Bailey was a mate, someone he could rely on. I know he blames himself for not seeing Bailey for who he really was, but how could he? Bailey was an expert at keeping secrets.

I turn to Sloane. 'You okay?'

'Yep. He won't last in there. Prisoners don't take kindly to men who abduct children. I find some peace in that.'

I nod, although I'm not sure I entirely agree with her eye-for-an-eye sense of justice. I just want answers.

'Do you think he gave them the names of who he was working with?' I ask.

She shrugs. 'Who knows. But hopefully whatever he shared it keeps some kids who were otherwise in danger safe with their parents.'

We sit in silence after that. How many others like Bailey are there out there? Sloane had found out the night he was arrested that Bailey had inherited his father's criminal activity—this had been going on for years. There could be hundreds of people part of the organisation, hundreds of kids being tracked, snatched.

How do we know who we can trust?

How am I ever supposed to take my eyes off my children?

# Chapter 37

## Amalia

### Twelve months later

I wake early. It's my favourite day of the week: Friday. Paul brings Lila to visit me every Friday morning. They always bring a new book to read and a trashy magazine. They are two of the very few approved items that I'm allowed to accept in prison.

A few months ago, my case went before the court and I was found guilty of kidnapping Imogen. However, due to the circumstances, my sentence was pretty light. This was my first offence (to their knowledge) and the police prosecution agreed that I was under a lot of stress with my own child missing, presumed dead. Lila starts kindergarten in a few weeks and I should be out of here by the time she starts school.

Bailey McDonald, on the other hand, will be in the slammer a lot longer. And so he should be. He kidnapped all those children, including my Lila, with the intention of selling them off to the highest bidder.

His accomplices are still at large. Bailey negotiated his sentence down by offering information, but the other guys were long gone by the time the cops got there—or at least that's what the media wants us to believe. Makes me sick they've gotten away with it while I sit here, separated from my baby girl. We did learn how we were targeted, though. It was through Paul's business social media page where he had shared a photo of Lila at Christmas.

I shower, dress and eat my breakfast. Just as I do every day. I don't make eye contact with anyone. I don't have friends to sit with. I keep my eyes down. I figure this is the best way to stay out of trouble. I don't need a reason to find myself in here a day longer than necessary.

At nine, the approved child visits begin and I sit in my cell, waiting impatiently to be collected.

'Mummy!' The sweetest voice in the world fills my ears as I enter the visiting area. It's like a tonic every time I hear it and it's enough to get me through the next week in this place.

'Hey, Lil! Hey, babe.' I grin at them both. 'I hear someone starts kindergarten next week.'

Lila nods her head excitedly.

'Are you all ready to start?'

'Yes. We got a new backpack and lunchbox and look, look.' Lila kicks her foot in the air, showing off a shiny new pair of sneakers. 'I run fast in these,' she adds.

'Wow! You're going to have so much fun running around kinder in those.'

We spend the next ten minutes discussing her backpack, lunchbox and what delicious treats Paul has promised to put in there. My heart aches. I'd often thought about what I'd pack in her lunchbox when she started kinder and school. I imagined the day I'd drop her off and take photos and meet her teacher. The evenings at home when she'd tell us about her day. Now we're going to have to cram a whole week of stories into these short, monitored sessions.

I swallow the lump in my throat.

'You okay?' Paul asks.

I wipe my eyes quickly and smile. 'Of course.'

'Lil, can you go and get me a cup of water from the fountain over there?' he asks.

She jumps up and does as she's told.

'Really?' he presses.

I sigh. 'I'm just devastated to be missing all of this.'

His brow furrows. 'I know. But I promise, I will take so many photos and we've already been keeping a diary of stories so that you can read about it when you get out. You'll catch up on it all. And then make more memories.'

I brush another tear away just as Lila returns, clutching a cup of water in both hands.

'Thank you,' Paul says, planting a kiss on top of her head.

'Are you sad, Mummy?'

'Just a little bit. I wish I could be at kinder on your first day.'

There's a moment of silence while Lila appears to think about that.

Her eyes light up all of a sudden. 'I know what we can do. I'll draw a picture of you and put it in my new backpack and you can come.'

A sob escapes me and this time I can't hide it. 'That's a beautiful idea. I'd love that.'

Like every Friday, the session ends too quickly. I stare at Lila until she's out of sight, hoping to burn every detail of her into my memory to last me until the next time I see her.

Once I'm back in my cell, I sit on my bed and look at the handful of photographs I'm permitted to keep.

I'd never have gotten her back if I didn't do what I did so I don't regret the actions that put me here. I'd do it again in a heartbeat. But I do regret taking my eyes off Lila that day the truck came. *You weren't watching*: that thought haunts me every day.

I'll be out of here in a year and then I'll make up for every lost moment with Lil.

# Epilogue

I scroll through the Word document, hoping the soft clicks of the computer mouse don't wake the child sleeping soundly next to me.

It's taken me more than twelve months to put this together. Late night after late night collecting articles, trawling through courtroom transcripts, compiling journals of my own conversations with witnesses.

Ideally, I would have an evidence wall with all my information laid out, red string pinned down, showing links between what I've discovered. But this project is my secret. It's like an illicit affair. I don't want anything printed off and left about to show what I've been doing this past year. I've already been accused of obsessing over the Rosewood child-trafficking ring. *Nonsense.* I'm a parent. It'd be negligent of me *not* to obsess over it. It's been almost two years since Bailey was arrested and there hasn't been a peep from the police about who he was working with or what they're doing to stop it happening again.

The little body next to me stretches out and I hold my breath. *Don't wake up. Don't wake up.*

Not tonight.

Not when I've finally had a breakthrough. One of the last pieces sliding into a jigsaw puzzle. I'm not finished but there's enough there that the end is in sight. Just a few pieces to go.

A photo—grainy, but enough. An address. A first name.

Footsteps pad down the hall and I look up to see Sam, eyes half-closed.

'Asleep?' they ask, glancing down at our child.

'Yep,' I reply, placing a shushing finger to my lips.

'Are you coming to bed soon?' I know Sam's frustrated with my late nights but I'm doing this for our children. Someone has to protect them.

'I just need another hour,' I say.

'Iris.' Their voice is so sharp I'm worried it'll wake Lara next to me. 'The twins are finally sleeping through and now *you're* staying up to ridiculous hours. You need to sleep.'

I sigh and close my laptop with an emphatic click.

'Thank you,' they say, shuffling back to our bedroom.

I scoop Lara up off the couch, careful not to wake her, and manage to successfully transfer her into her bed.

My mind races as I crawl under the covers next to Sam. I wish I could tell them what I've discovered, but they won't understand. Not everything I've collected has been done so entirely legally. I've had to steal, hack—footage, text messages, emails. Who knew listening to so many true crime podcasts and watching so many serial killer docuseries would make me such a sleuth?

The problem is, I can't take what I've got to the police, and I can't tell Sam.

I have to do this on my own.

# Acknowledgments

Firstly, thank you to my readers for taking the time to read *You Weren't Watching*. I was overwhelmed by the love and support for *While the Baby Sleeps* and it was you guys who made this book possible. You allow me to keep doing the thing I love.

Thank you to Kylie Mason, for helping me redraft this beauty to make it what it is and to Penny Carroll for your incredible editing skills.

Thank you Elle Maxwell for your design expertise and creating the perfect cover to complement the first.

Thank you Deb for being one of my beta readers and the biggest thanks to Elle and Bec who have each read this at least three times and who give me so much of their time listening to my questions, stresses and celebrations.

Thanks Emma, Elle and Ali who give me a hit of energy and laughter everyday, and who I can rely on to be my personal cheerleaders when I'm in the pits of self-doubt.

Thank you Jen for your medical expertise and for your inspiration as a first responder in real-life.

Finally, thank you to my family and especially Jason and Mum who give me kid-free time to get creative.

# About Author

Stephanie Hazeltine is a contemporary fiction author who writes about fearless females as they fall in love, navigate motherhood or tackle mysteries.

She lives in Melbourne, Australia with her husband, two kids and two cavoodles.

*Sign up to her mailing list to be the first to know about new releases and exclusive news.*

Website: www.stephaniehazeltine.com

Instagram: @stephaniehazeltinewrites

TikTok: @stephaniehazeltinewrites

# Also By Stephanie Hazeltine

*While the Baby Sleeps* - The prequel to You Weren't Watching. Read
it <u>now</u>

*Anyone But Him* - a spicy, enemies-to-lovers collection of novellas.

Read it <u>now</u>